"Nash—"

He shushed her with a finger over her lips. "You have the most beautiful mouth I've ever seen on a woman. When I'm alone in this room with you, and the rest of the world is some distant nightmare outside that door, all I can think about is that kiss we shared yesterday."

"You were delirious with fever. You probably aren't remembering it accurately."

At last those firm lips crooked up with a dangerous grin. "How's my temperature now, Nurse Rodriguez?"

"Normal. Your fever hasn't come back." Was that hushed quiver of anticipation really coming from her throat?

Nash brushed the calloused pad of his thumb across her bottom lip, sparking a dozen different nerve endings. "My eyes are focused? My thoughts are sane? No delusions?"

Her mouth was parched with anticipation. "As far as I can tell, you're...healthy."

"Good. I just wanted to make sure we're clear on this." Then he leaned in, replacing his thumb with his mouth.

CROSSFIRE CHRISTMAS

USA TODAY **Bestselling Author**

JULIE MILLER

HARLEQUIN® INTRIGUE®

For the cast and crew of Grand Island Little Theater's production of *Twelve Angry Men*.

I don't think I've ever been prouder of a show I've directed.

With particular thanks to Jeremy Johnson and Liz Boyle for the title idea for this book!

ISBN-13: 978-0-373-69797-7

Crossfire Christmas

Copyright © 2014 by Julie Miller

Recycling programs for this product may not exist in your area.

Printed in U.S.A.

www.Harlequin.com

ABOUT THE AUTHOR

USA TODAY bestselling author Julie Miller attributes her passion for writing romance to all those books she read growing up. When shyness and asthma kept her from becoming the action-adventure heroine she longed to be, Julie created stories in her head to keep herself entertained. Encouragement from her family to write down the feelings and ideas she couldn't express became a love for the written word. She gets continued support from her fellow members of the Prairieland Romance Writers, where this teacher serves as the resident "grammar goddess." Inspired by the likes of Agatha Christie and Encyclopedia Brown, Julie believes the only thing better than a good mystery is a good romance.

Born and raised in Missouri, this award-winning author now lives in Nebraska with her husband, son and an assortment of spoiled pets. To contact Julie or to learn more about her books, write to P.O. Box 5162, Grand Island, NE 68802-5162 or check out her website and monthly newsletter at www.juliemiller.org.

Books by Julie Miller

HARLEQUIN INTRIGUE

CAST OF CHARACTERS

Agent Charles Nash—When this Texas DEA agent's cover is blown, he vows to find out the truth about who murdered his fellow agents and marked him for death. Wounded and alone in a city he doesn't know, he kidnaps the beautiful nurse who stops to help him. Before long, the only ones they can trust are each other.

Teresa Rodriguez—When a sexy cowboy kidnaps her at gunpoint and forces her to treat his wounds, she's plunged into a perilous adventure. But her captor quickly becomes her hero when he saves her life. Feeling a pull toward this man, she makes a dangerous deal—keep him alive until he can find answers, then he'll let her go home for Christmas. Surviving the holidays will be hard enough. Guarding her heart? Impossible.

Berto Graciela—The crime boss will make any deal necessary to secure his position as heir to his brother's drug cartel.

Santiago Vargas—The Graciela lieutenant is challenging Berto's claim to power. And he's bringing the turf war to Kansas City.

Laila Alvarez—A very brave little girl.

Captain Jesse Puente—Nash's superior officer in Houston.

Agent Cruz Moreno—Brand-new to Nash's team. Can this hotshot be trusted?

Agent Tommy Delvecchio—Like a kid brother to Nash. He wasn't ready to be a field agent.

Angel and Julian Sanchez—For the right price, these brothers will kill anyone.

Chapter One

"You're a dead man, Nash!"

DEA agent Charlie Nash slammed his back against the metal shelves that had blocked the spray of bullets and saved his life. One step slower and he'd be bleeding out on the floor like the young man lying in the open aisle beside Thug One.

"Kid?" He wasn't really expecting a response.

He didn't get one. Check one more black mark in the loss column of his soul.

Yet there was no time for guilt or regret or even grief. He'd spotted the trap the moment he'd pulled into the parking garage and would have backed out then, evading the threat that had trailed him seven hundred miles from Texas to Kansas City, Missouri. But with the rookie handler climbing out of his car without a clue, Nash had been left with no choice but to stay put and warn the young agent back into his vehicle.

Revealing himself to the three goons lying in wait hadn't made a damn bit of difference.

The kid was still dead.

And he was still the Graciela cartel's most wanted man.

The cop who'd put together the plan to stop them.

Nash pulled a bandanna from the back pocket of his

jeans and tied it around his left thigh, trying to slow down the blood seeping from the wound there. As he tightened the makeshift bandage, he listened to the clomp of running feet, pinpointing the locations of the two remaining assailants as they tried to flank him. He ignored the throbbing burn in his leg and fought to calm his labored breathing so the clouds of stress and exertion in the open warehouse's wintry air wouldn't give his position away. He figured he had about two minutes—three if he was lucky—to find a way out of this mess.

The desk agent who'd met him in this run-down auto-parts warehouse near the Missouri River to try to help him reestablish his undercover persona hadn't been so lucky. He'd wager most of the car parts in this place weren't legal, and that Tommy Delvecchio had never been in the middle of a real firefight before. Stupid kid must not have been wearing his flak vest, judging by the size of that puddle of blood pooling beneath him.

If Delvecchio had been one of Nash's operatives, he'd have trained him better than that. Hell. If he'd been one of Nash's undercover operatives, he'd probably still be dead. Just like the other embedded agents whose covers had been blown.

Glancing over at the still figure crumpled on the floor between storage racks, Nash felt his gut twist with anger and remorse. "Damn it, Tommy. Told you I didn't need backup." All he'd asked for was cash and a new ID to be sent to a PO box. He hadn't needed a personal delivery. He hadn't wanted the kid to come all the way to K.C. "You should have stayed at the office."

You can't risk hiding out for more than forty-eight hours, boss. And you said you can't trust anyone in the field. You need someone who isn't part of the Graciela-Vargas turf war to do this for you. Nash could imagine

Agent Delvecchio rising to attention beside his computer, eager to get on the next flight to KCI and prove himself. *I'm not a field agent. They don't know me. I can help.*

Smart kid. Good logic. Still dead. Just like Torres and Richter back in Harlingen and Houston. Nash's team was another man down, he had no ID on the traitor who'd marked them as cops, and he was on his own in this nightmare.

Pushing aside the distracting emotions that could get him killed, too, Nash quickly evaluated his options. The stinging smell of sulfur in the air told him the three shooters—down to two now—had used up a lot of their bullets coming after him and Delvecchio. But that didn't give him the advantage it should have.

He kicked out the magazine from his Smith & Wesson and checked his own ammo supply before reloading the clip. Three bullets left. The rest of the ammunition and backup weaponry he needed were in the go bag lying on the floor beside Delvecchio. The only chance of a getaway was his truck, parked a good thirty yards from his position. And as far as he could tell, there were still two of Berto Graciela's thugs in the warehouse with him.

Unless these were Santiago Vargas's men. Vargas had been loyal to Berto's older brother, Diego. Ever since Diego's death two years earlier, the two had been vying for power within the organization. What did a few cops mean to either of them? Just collateral damage in a war to control a drug-trafficking pipeline that funneled cocaine, pot and an assortment of designer concoctions across the border—or straight into the U.S. at import traffic hubs like Houston, K.C. and Chicago.

But Nash's team had been making progress. They'd fed the DEA precious intel, helping the agency shut down some key distribution centers. Now Nash and his men were dying.

How had they found him here in Kansas City? Who had found him? He was over ten hours away from his last encounter with Graciela's men in Houston. Had they followed the kid? If so, how had they connected computer geek Thomas Delvecchio to him? Was there a hidden tracking device on his Ford F-250 he'd missed? Unlikely. He'd gone over the thing with a fine-tooth comb at a truck stop in Tulsa, Oklahoma, the last time he'd checked in with his captain in the Houston office and made the arrangements with Delvecchio.

There had to be a leak somewhere in the system. One of the DEA's confidential informants wasn't keeping things so confidential. Torres or Richter had let something slip in the wrong place at the wrong time. Or worst-case scenario? One of Graciela's or Vargas's men had infiltrated the Houston office and Nash's men were at the mercy of a double agent.

That had to be the answer. A team didn't lose three agents in a week unless someone was leaking inside information.

"You're outnumbered, Señor Nash!" one of the thugs taunted, his accent rolling his *R*s and making the gibe sound like a joke instead of a promise of death. "You are the mouse and we are the *gatos*. When you come out of your hole, we'll be waiting to pounce."

So at least one man had taken up position near the open garage door.

Time to stop speculating about who had betrayed him and deal with the threat at hand. Nash craned his neck to peer through a stack of sports car bumpers to gauge the distance and amount of open ground he'd have to cover before reaching his truck.

On a good day, he could do it in a matter of seconds. But this was far from a good day. And he didn't have a location on the second shooter.

Time to go old school.

After slipping off the black felt Stetson that the years had shaped so perfectly to his head, he kissed the crown and set it on the shelf beside him, nudging it into clear view near the end of the row. Then he pushed to his feet and pulled down the pile of bumpers, creating a noisy diversion while he ducked into the next aisle and ran for his truck.

Boom. His hat flew off the shelf, giving him a twenty on Thug Three. The angle of that last shot told Nash the man was running parallel through the stacks with him.

Well, *running* was a relative term. Thug Three was an overweight man who moved with the grace of a lumbering buffalo, while Nash was hobbled by the wound on his leg.

But Nash was still faster.

Sorry, kid. I owe you one. He scooped up the heavy nylon go bag from the floor beside Delvecchio and limped toward the open garage area with a galloping gait. Twenty yards. Fifteen. He could feel the blood running down his leg and filling his left boot. Thank God the shot hadn't taken out his knee or ankle.

Ten yards.

The damp wind and flakes of blowing snow pelted his face as he broke into the open garage area.

Ah, hell.

Thug Two stepped out from behind a rolling toolbox and shot at him. Either the guy had piss-poor aim or Nash was lurching on his gimpy leg more than he thought. One bullet smacked into the side of the truck bed, punching a hole through the black metal. The second shot went wide and shattered the driver's-side window.

Nash raised his gun and squeezed the trigger.

Thug Two didn't get off a third shot.

Nash swore when Thug Three stumbled out from shelves near the dead body by the garage door. Couldn't a guy catch a break? Nash swept the broken glass off his seat, tossed the bag into the truck and climbed in behind the wheel. The big man silhouetted against the sunny glare of the snow outside was panting hard. But he wasn't relying on perfect aim to stop Nash. He pulled out a second handgun and fired both in a smoky barrage of sparks and firepower.

Nash started the engine and stuck his left hand out the broken window. Bracing his wrist on the mirror to steady his aim, he pulled the trigger. With a flurry of Spanish curses, Thug Three dropped one of his weapons and shook his fingers. Lucky shot. Nash must have hit the gun and stung his hand.

But two shots and he was done. No way could he reach his bag on the floorboards across the truck and reload in time. Dropping the gun into his lap, Nash shifted the truck into Drive. He'd only irritated Thug Three. The big man clasped both hands around his remaining weapon and fired.

Nash stomped on the accelerator. A bullet smacked the windshield on the passenger side, splintering the glass into a web of cracks. The wheels spun until they found traction on the smooth concrete. A second bullet took out his side mirror. The truck lurched forward and barreled toward the exit. A third bullet found the open window and ripped through his left shoulder, spinning downward through the muscle, oblivious to the protective vest he wore.

The explosion of pain in his shoulder and back was instant and intense. Damn lucky shot robbed him of breath and jerked his grip on the wheel, sending the truck into a sideways skid. Squeezing his elbow to his side, Nash collapsed into the steering wheel, hugging his right arm around it—regaining control of the truck and making himself a smaller target. He was close enough to see the yellowed teeth of Thug Three's smile as the man steadied the gun and took aim at Nash's head.

But what good ol' Texas boy didn't know how to play chicken?

"For Tommy," Nash wheezed, stomping on the accelerator. Before Thug Three could pull off the kill shot or dive out of the way, Nash plowed into him.

With a sickening double jolt, the truck bounced over the body and burst into the sunshine of the clear December afternoon. Nash raced away from the warehouse, clipping a couple of junker cars and jumping the curb out of the back alley before pulling onto the street.

"Brilliant plan, Nash," he muttered through gritted teeth as he slowed to merge with a line of cars. His entire left side was on fire and the pain doubled every time he tried to catch a deep breath. No way to tell yet if the bullet had gone through or had clipped a lung and was bouncing around inside him. But he knew from the lightheaded haze he had to shake off that he was losing a lot of blood. Delvecchio was dead and, like him, any hope that Nash had escaped to Kansas City undetected had literally been shot to hell. He was no closer to finding out the identity of the traitor who had exposed his men as undercover cops and marked them, and now him, for death.

Worse, he was on his own. He'd better report in to Captain Puente and tell him he was going off the grid until further notice. No more help from the remnants of his team. No more deaths on his conscience. He wasn't putting any more of his people in the line of fire until he could figure this thing out.

Nash slowed to a stop at a traffic light and unsnapped the cell phone on his belt. After wiping away the clammy sweat that dotted his forehead, he searched the screen for Jesse Puente's office line, punched it in and tucked the phone between his ear and shoulder so he could twist around and untie the blood-soaked bandanna on his thigh.

The light turned green before the number picked up.

"Captain?" Nash dropped the bandanna in his lap and gripped the wheel again as he pressed on the accelerator. The responding silence raised every suspicious hackle Nash possessed. Puente liked the sound of his own voice too much for him not to start talking. "Who's this?"

"Agent Cruz Moreno, Drug Enforcement Agency, Houston office." Like Nash, the officer spoke with a hint of suspicion coloring his tone. "Who is this? How did you get this number?"

A quick grunt of relief clouded the cold air leaching in through the truck's shattered window. Cruz Moreno was the newest man Puente had recruited. He'd transferred over from the San Antonio office and was being trained to replace the slain officers working in the Graciela organization. Thank God Nash had convinced Captain Puente to hold off sending Moreno into the field. Although not as green as Tommy had been, he wasn't up to speed yet on the intricacies of their long-term investigation. "This is Nash. Put the captain on."

"Puente isn't here right now." Urgency replaced the caution in Moreno's tone. "Where are you, man? The captain booked it out of here as soon as we lost contact with Delvecchio's phone. Tommy missed his call-in time. Did you two meet up?"

Nash pulsed his grip on the wheel, his body feeling hot and chilled at the same time. And it wasn't just his injuries messing with his ability to focus right now. "Tommy's dead."

"Dead? I knew that kid couldn't—" Moreno's bilingual curses pretty much summed up the grief and rage Nash felt. "I'm calling Puente on the other line. You need backup? An extraction?"

"No. I need to disappear. I need time to find this guy before he finds me. I'm gonna put a stop to this." Nash released the steering wheel at the next stop and wadded up the bandanna to stuff it beneath his vest to stanch the wound. Pain knifed through him at the added pressure and he swore. "Tell Puente he can claim Tommy's body in Kansas City."

"Is that where you are?"

The agonizing jolt cleared his head for a split second, and Nash got the feeling he'd already said too much. Someone had leaked his name, along with Torres's, Richter's and Delvecchio's, to Graciela's or Vargas's men. That someone could be listening in on the line right now. And even though Cruz wore the same badge Nash did, trusting anyone—even a fellow agent—just wasn't going to happen. "Not anymore, Moreno. I'm halfway to Chicago," Nash lied, wondering how far away he could get before another thug or the hole in his chest stopped him. "I'll call again when it's safe. Until then, I'm going off the grid."

"What about backup?"

No. Solo was the only way to go until he knew who was killing his team. "If I'm as good at this job as I hope I am, I won't need it."

Bold words for a man whose left hand was going numb

inside his glove and whose sheer will was keeping him upright.

"We've got no idea who's behind this yet, so watch your back, Nash."

"You, too."

He could hear Captain Puente's voice in the background, grousing on the other line as Moreno gave him a brief sit rep. Then Cruz was back, no doubt relaying a message. "Is this phone clean?"

"What?"

"Are you using the burner phone Tommy brought you? If Graciela's men could track Tommy, then chances are they can locate you, too."

Nash cursed. *Rookie mistake.* "I'm done."

"Wait. The captain wants to know where in Chicago—?"

But Nash had already disconnected the call. He raised his aching leg to guide the wheel on the straight stretch of road, freeing his good hand to turn off the phone and raise it to his teeth to pry open the back. He pulled out the battery and GPS chip and spit them out on the seat beside him, going dark on any kind of satellite trace. Unfortunately, though, that meant he had no means of communication on him, either, until he could find a spot to stop where a bleeding man in a broken truck wouldn't draw attention, and he could unpack the new phone in his go bag.

And since he was clearly off his game, Nash had driven into the heart of downtown instead of catching one of the highways and had the dumb luck to be caught in the heart of rush-hour traffic. Until he could get his bearings, until he could think this whole mess through and decide where he needed to go, he'd just keep driving.

He'd come to K.C. to hook up with an old friend, Jake

Lonergan, a former agent who'd gotten out of the business. He'd hoped for a spare bed or sofa to bunk on for a night or two until he could make some inquiries and form a new plan of action. But Jake had a family now, complete with a wife and little girl, and another baby on the way. Nash seriously doubted his old friend would appreciate him bringing a drug war to his front doorstep.

He'd met a couple of guys at KCPD a little over a year ago, working on another case. But they weren't the kind of buddies a desperate man called on for off-the-record help. He'd trusted every man on his team—would have called Torres or Richter in a heartbeat. But now they were gone. Besides, he didn't want to be responsible for the deaths of any more cops. Whether the Graciela-Vargas war had extended its reach to Kansas City or they'd come here just for him, he could imagine they wouldn't take too kindly to interference from anyone else who wore a badge.

Nash slowed his truck and followed the flow of traffic through a fancy shopping district decorated with more lights than he could count and window displays for the upcoming holiday. He hadn't even thought about Christmas. Besides the fact his parents were gone and he had no siblings and was married to his work, he'd been too busy trying to stop the drugs and save his team these past few months. Celebrating the holidays was for men with families and kids who still believed in the kind of magic and hope he'd stopped believing in long ago.

Right now he just had to live long enough to ID a traitor and exact a little revenge on the man who'd sentenced his agent brothers to death. Legally, if he could. But a bullet to the head would be justice enough if he couldn't find any other way to finish this.

Maybe he'd see Christmas next week. If he was lucky,

he'd see New Year's. He glanced down at the blood seeping through the hole in his leather coat.

Or maybe, if he didn't clear his head and think of some options fast, he wouldn't even live to see tomorrow.

"FINALLY. HERE'S THE horse I've been looking for."

Teresa Rodriguez watched Laila Alvarez sag into her wheelchair, dropping the scissors and magazine she held into her lap. Despite the little girl's brave smile and never-ending chatter, Teresa could tell that thirty minutes of making ornaments in the playroom of the Truman Medical Center's children's wing had taxed the eight-year-old's energy.

Knowing her patients better than they sometimes knew themselves, Teresa slipped her hand over the glue stick on the table and dropped it into the pocket of her cartoon-print scrub jacket before Laila noticed. She nodded toward the image of a team of brown-and-white horses. "Those are Clydesdales. They grow big and strong and pull heavy wagons. They'll be a nice addition to your stable."

"Are they bigger than you?"

At five foot three, Teresa found that a lot of things, except her patients, were taller than her. "Bigger than you and me both." She leaned in with a smile and gently took the magazine and scissors from her young friend. "How about I set the Clydesdale aside, and we can cut him out and put him on a new ornament tomorrow."

Laila closed her fingers in a halfhearted grab. "But I want to finish decorating the tree." She gazed longingly over at the Christmas tree in front of the bank of windows. An Appaloosa, a buckskin, a pinto, a palomino and a Lipizzaner stallion already hung from yarn bows in the branches, along with ornaments other children had made. "And I want one to hang in my room."

"I said we could work until we ran out of supplies, remember?" Teresa gestured to the tabletop. "We're out of glue. I'll have to get some more on my way home. But we'll finish them later. I promise."

Despite the wistful expression in her cocoa-brown eyes, Laila nodded. She moved her small fingers to the picture of a barn and hay bales that she'd already glued to a piece of cardboard for Teresa to cut out and string a loop of yarn through. "I need a cowboy to watch the horses for me when I'm not here."

"After I get the glue, I'll go by a bookstore and find a magazine with lots of cowboys in it to bring to the hospital."

"You're the best nurse ever, Teresa," Laila gushed on little more than a whisper.

Teresa smoothed her hand over the knit cap that covered the girl's bald head. "You're the best patient, sweetie." With a quick glance at her watch, Teresa rose and turned Laila's chair toward the hallway. "Come on. Let's get you back to your room. It's time for your medication, and I think maybe you can use a nap."

"But I—"

"You want to be fresh and smiling when your mom and dad come in after work, don't you?"

Laila nodded. "Can we show them the ornaments I hung up?"

"Absolutely." Teresa parked her friend at the central desk to chat with an aide and a receptionist while she went into the dispensary and unlocked the prescribed medication. Then she wheeled her patient through the wide door to her room and locked the chair beside the bed before helping the determined girl stand and climb beneath the covers herself.

Teresa handed Laila the stuffed horse from her bedside table and the little girl hugged the well-loved toy to her chest while she chewed her tablets. After giving her charge a sip of water and tucking her in, Teresa checked the girl's vitals and recorded the details and medication on her computer tablet. Laila was asleep before she was done.

"Oh, sweetie." With a smile that was part admiration and part heartache, Teresa caught her long ponytail behind her neck and leaned over to kiss the girl's pale cheek. Then she closed the blinds, unlocked the wheelchair and headed back into the hallway.

Returning to the playroom, Teresa quickly cleaned up their mess and pulled over an ottoman to set Laila's artwork safely out of the way on the top shelf of the supply cabinet. As she climbed down to return the glue stick to a lower shelf, she made a mental list of other craft supplies they were running low on that she could pick up to keep the children who visited siblings or were patients here entertained. She suspected that Laila and a few of the other long-term care patients would be here over Christmas next week. Maybe she'd add some small gifts for them to her shopping list, too. Plan a party. Bring decorations from home to add more holiday color to their sterile environment. She had a couple of days off she could spend shopping, decorating and wrapping gifts. She glanced toward the waning sun and white flakes floating past the windows and grinned. If she cleared it with the doctors, maybe she could even bring the ingredients to help the children make snow ice cream.

No one should have to be alone on Christmas Day, denied the family and fun of the blessed celebration. No one should have to be sick or injured and in the hospital, either.

Humming a tune at the plan that was coming together in her head, Teresa locked things up and headed back to the nurse's station to update her end-of-day reports. Although it had nothing to do with physical care, putting together a holiday party for the patients in the children's wing would do wonders to raise their spirits. That was probably why she'd become a nurse instead of the artist she'd originally intended to be in college. Teresa was hardwired to help anyone in need. She needed to make a difference in other people's lives.

Even if all she could do was make a little girl with a brain tumor forget her surgeries for a few minutes and bring a smile to her face at Christmastime, she was going to do it.

"There you are."

Teresa looked up from her laptop to see a petite woman with dark brown hair and cheekbones that matched her own waddling up to the counter.

"Emilia." She quickly stood to greet her oldest sister. The white coat and shadows beneath her eyes told Teresa that Dr. Emilia Rodriguez-Grant had just finished a long shift in the E.R.—if she wasn't still on duty. "What brings you to the third floor?"

"Have you looked out the windows?" Emilia pointed to the bank of glass in the playroom before bringing her hands back to rub at her pregnant belly and the small of her back. "We're supposed to get three to five more inches of snow on top of what's already on the ground tonight."

Here we go again.

Teresa inhaled a steadying breath but couldn't keep

the sarcasm out of her voice. "It's December in Missouri? Snow happens."

"Don't get smart with me." Emilia tugged a lock of her recently bobbed hair behind her ear, practically clucking like a mother hen. "It'll be dark soon. But the sun was bright enough today to melt some of the snow. You know when the temperatures drop, it will refreeze into ice. Driving will be very dangerous."

Although she would've liked to blame this overprotective streak on Emilia's pregnancy and the fact their mother had passed away just over a year ago, Teresa was far too familiar with her older sibling's smothering concerns. It was both a blessing and a curse to be part of such a tight-knit, loving family. While she knew she was loved and would never lack for someone to care about her, she was the baby of the family, and asserting her independence was a challenge she'd been working on for most of her twenty-nine years.

"Thanks for the weather report. But I've been driving since I was sixteen—in worse conditions than this. I'll be fine."

"You know we promised Mama we'd look out for you." Why hadn't that dictate been given regarding any of her older sisters and brother? Maybe their father's murder when she was a baby or the fact she'd been mugged her first summer out of high school or having a veteran cop for a big brother made them all unusually cautious about protecting their own. Still, it would be nice if one day her brother and sisters would see her as an equal adult and not that fatherless baby or traumatized teen. "I want you to head for home as soon as your shift is done," Emilia cautioned.

Teresa risked a little nudge toward independence. "I

need to pick up some groceries. And I was planning to do a little Christmas shopping."

"Teresa—"

"Then I'm going straight to my apartment to bake cookies for Laila and the other pediatric patients to decorate. What kind of trouble can I get into buying baking goods and Christmas gifts?"

Emilia arched a dark brow. *"Gamberro—"* aka Troublemaker "—is your middle name, Teresa." She tempered her skepticism with a smile and a hug. "Just remember you can call any of us if you have a problem with your car or the roads. I don't want you stranded out in the cold."

Were any of her older siblings getting the same lecture? Of course, they all had spouses and children at home expecting their arrival, who'd worry if they didn't show up at a certain place at a certain time. Teresa didn't even have a cat waiting for her at her apartment. She should be more appreciative of their concern.

"I won't be. But just in case, I've got an emergency kit in my trunk, complete with blankets and flares, and I'll keep my cell phone in my pocket." Teresa tightened her arms briefly around her sister, then pulled back to touch Emilia's distended belly. "Now you go home and get off your feet. Hug Justin and my nephew and get yourself and this little one some rest."

The tension in her sister's face eased as she placed her hand beside Teresa's. "I think this one is going to be like her *tía* Teresa."

"Pretty and smart?"

Emilia laughed. "A handful. I swear this one tosses and turns twenty-four hours a day. Not at all like when I was pregnant with her big brother."

Teresa sobered with concerns of her own. "Do you

need me to drive you home? Is your blood pressure spiking again?"

"No, no." Really? Her family wouldn't even let her do this little thing? "Justin is coming by the hospital to get me after he picks up Joey from day care. I'm fine. You just take care of yourself. Unless you want Justin to drive you home, too?"

Teresa bit down on her frustration and summoned a smile for her sister. "No, thanks. I'll be fine."

Emilia cupped Teresa's cheek before turning away. "Have you decided what you're doing for the holiday yet?"

"I'm planning a Christmas party for the children here the afternoon of the twenty-fifth."

"I mean Christmas morning. It would be fun for all of us to help with your party later in the day. We could make extra food and bring gifts. Joey and our nieces and nephews would have fun playing with the boys and girls here." Teresa knew that look—the one that said *I love you* and *You'll need our help* at the same time. "But you'll be joining us all at AJ and Claire's to unwrap presents and eat brunch, right?"

Teresa understood mixed emotions all too well. Just as much as she loved her family, she wanted them to respect her skills and maturity and desire to be who she needed to be. But that battle was for another time. Not the holidays.

Her answer was sincere. "I wouldn't miss it for the world."

Chapter Two

Nash couldn't remember how long he'd been driving, and he had no clue where the highway was taking him.

Shaking off the fogginess in his head, he pulled off the next exit ramp and drove through some cookie-cutter neighborhood mecca. The front yards were dotted with wire reindeer and giant inflatable lawn ornaments. The snow and suburbia were as foreign to him as the need to find an ally who could help him.

He blinked away the frost forming on his eyelashes as his brain skipped from one random thought to the next. It was freaking cold here in Missouri; he had no driver's-side window to roll up and he'd lost his hat. He loved that hat. It was a sentimental homage to the boys ranch where he'd lived and worked and gone to school after his parents' deaths at the hands of a pair of drugged-up teenagers who'd invaded their home. Nash had grown up and taken a job with the DEA to combat the flow of drugs into Texas and other parts of the U.S., to stop another tragedy like his parents' murders, to help troubled kids like he'd been find a healthier way to deal with the crap life threw at them.

He usually oversaw or handled undercover operations where an agent infiltrated a gang or cartel or independent meth lab to gather information to stop the drugs being made, trafficked or sold. But two of his agents had been exposed as cops and killed. So he'd gone undercover himself to find out how and why and who and had ended up with too many suspects and too little concrete evidence.

Somehow, Berto Graciela had found out he was a cop, too.

He was driving in circles.

Tommy Delvecchio was dead.

"Ah, hell." A moment of painful clarity put the brakes on Nash's rambling thoughts.

He'd come to Kansas City with one desperate plan in mind. Without knowing who'd betrayed him in Houston, he'd gone elsewhere to find a sanctuary where he could lie low long enough to safely figure out his next move.

He reconsidered calling Jake Lonergan, who'd left the DEA due to a nearly fatal head injury that had robbed him of his memory. Jake probably didn't want any part of the violence chasing Nash to enter his happily-ever-after life. But, sitting in a pool of his own blood and panting for nearly every breath, Nash knew his luck was running out. It might cost him a friendship, but Jake was all he had left.

Taking his hand off the reloaded gun at his side, Nash brushed the snow off his lap at the next stoplight and reached inside the bag Tommy had brought him to pull out the untraceable phone. Even that subtle shift in his seat renewed the pain like a stab in the back. Thug One had winged him in the leg, creating a discomfort he could simply throw a bandage over. But Thug Three had got him good. He still couldn't tell if the bullet had gone through or if it was lodged inside him somewhere. All he knew was that he was hurt. He was bleeding. And he wasn't going to get any better on his own.

The light changed. A horn honked behind him before

Nash stepped on the accelerator and moved along with the traffic past a busy shopping mall and a modern hospital. He debated whether or not to turn off into the hospital's E.R. But if the men after him were smart—and clearly they were or they wouldn't have tracked him to K.C.— they'd be checking E.R.s across the city looking for him. Besides, a gunshot victim showing up in a hospital was an automatic call to the local police and a subsequent alert to the DEA office in Houston. That was the kind of publicity he didn't need. Until he knew who had set him up, trusting anyone, even a cop, wasn't a good idea.

When he reached the next crossroads, Nash spotted a narrow two-lane road leading away from the suburbs and turned. He needed to get someplace without all these cars and people—someplace where he could put the first-aid kit in his bag to good use without anyone trying to help him or ask any questions. He needed a place where he could pull off and make sense of the dancing letters and numerals on his phone as he tried to recall Jake Lonergan's number, which had been programmed into the phone he didn't want to reactivate.

The truck wheels spun on a patch of snow-packed road and he dropped his phone to grab the wheel and keep the big Ford from skidding across the asphalt. Coming from Houston, he wasn't used to driving in weather like this. Of course, if the world outside his cracked windshield hadn't been such a blur, and he hadn't been shivering from the icy wind blowing in through his busted window, he might have been able to handle the treacherous stretch of winding road he'd pulled off onto.

But he was hurt. He was bleeding. He was cold.

When he crested the hill and hit the next patch of black ice, Mother Nature finally did what a half dozen thugs in two different cities hadn't been able to do.

She took him out.

Nash's truck sailed off the shoulder of the road and plowed into the ditch. It careened up the other side and slammed into a tree. A wave of snow flew over the truck as he banged his head against something hard and blacked out.

TERESA DRUMMED HER gloved fingers against the steering wheel and hummed along with the Christmas music on the radio while she waited at the stoplight.

She tilted her gaze up to the big flakes of snow drifting from the charcoal sky into the light from the streetlamps. "See, Emilia?" She taunted the invisible big sister she felt arching a warning eyebrow over her shoulder. "Shopping's done. Traffic's fine and I'm on my way home with nary a problem whatsoever. And I did it all by my little lonesome."

Not like a couple hours of defiant refusal to heed Emilia's warning and go straight home in the nasty weather could really quell the nagging, indulgent voices of her siblings in her head.

You're so good with children, but if you want any of your own, you'll have to get serious about a man first. I'd already had Olivia and Maria by the time I was your age. A girl can't wait forever.

But she could wait for the right one.

My husband has a friend I want to introduce you to. He has a good job at the college business office and he's stable.

Dullsville. Sounded like another overprotective trap in the making.

You should move closer to us. They're building new condos across the street. And it's a better neighborhood.

She liked her apartment—had it decorated just the

way she wanted. The neighborhood might not be prime real estate, but there were some good people living in her building. Besides, big brother AJ had taught each of his sisters, wife and nieces the basics of self-defense and personal safety. She could take care of herself.

I don't want you driving without an emergency kit in your car, especially in winter. Flashlight? Jumper cables? Kitty litter? Make an appointment to get the tires rotated, too.

Done, done and done. Even before AJ, Emilia, Luisa or Ana had all mentioned reminders about winter driving safety to her.

Just because she longed for her family's respect for her choices and a little bit of independence in her life, didn't mean she was a naive fool. An optimist, yes. A resourceful go-getter. A hopeless holiday lover. But not a fool.

"Why can't they see that?"

The light turned green, and Teresa cranked up the radio, turning her thoughts to something more pleasant. Like sugar cookies. And wrapping gifts.

She drove through the intersection after the cars ahead of her turned off toward the highway, and she continued on to the back-road shortcut to her neighborhood. The busy roads and businesses open late for holiday shopping gave way to country homes on hilly acreages. Then civilization thinned out to a recycling center and a shooting range. Finally, she was winding through woods and farmland. She'd pass through about two miles of bare trees reaching up like dark, gnarled fingers in the foggy twilight and pretty hillsides of undisturbed snow.

Although the twisting road was more dangerous than the straight lanes of bypasses and city streets, she loved this drive, especially in the winter. When the stars were out and the moon was full, it could be as bright as all the holiday lights on the Plaza. And on cold, damp evenings like this, with big flakes of snow swirling in and out of the shadows, it conjured up images of gothic romance, with mysterious heroes, hidden castles and storm-swept moors.

Teresa was imagining a castle hidden behind the frosted branches of the trees when she crested the hill and saw the tire tracks cutting through the snow at the side of the road. Automatically, she pumped her brakes and slowed, peering over the edge of the blacktop.

"Oh, my God."

A silent alarm tightened her grip around the steering wheel. She braked again and pulled onto the shoulder for a closer look, angling her headlights toward the trees.

The tracks ran down into the ditch and up the next incline, leading to a black pickup truck that had finally been stopped short by the trunk of an old pine.

The truck's lights were on. The plume of exhaust making a black spot in the churned-up snow meant the engine was still running. The accident was recent. Or else the driver wasn't able to turn off the motor....

Gamberro is your middle name. Despite her sister's teasing, Teresa didn't believe she caused that much difficulty or misfortune. But she wasn't about to walk away from trouble like this when there was something she could do to help.

Teresa clicked on her hazard lights and pulled her cell phone from her pocket. She glanced ahead at the dark road. She checked the pavement behind her in her mirrors—equally dark. A curtain of falling snow seemed to mask her and the accident below from the rest of the world.

Had the driver called for help yet? Was he or she even able to call?

Taking a deep breath, Teresa pulled the hood of her parka up over her dark hair and unbuckled her seat belt. She pulled out the flashlight AJ had insisted she keep in her glove compartment and braced herself for the blast of winter outside. Deciding to leave the engine and heater running in case the driver was able to move and needed a warm place to sit and wait for a tow truck, she climbed out and circled to the front of her car.

Dots of blowing snow melted on her cheeks and nose and obscured her vision as she huddled inside her coat.

"Hello?" Her shout was swallowed up by the cold, damp air. Her flashlight was too small to pierce the gloom at this distance. "Is anyone in the truck?"

Her sigh formed a puffy cloud in the air. The snow was knee-deep for a woman who was only five-three. And even though she'd changed from her work clogs to wool-lined ankle boots, she knew they wouldn't be tall enough to get her past that first drift where the road crew had piled snow when they'd scraped the road.

"What's a little wet and cold, anyway?" she dared herself, tightening her scarf against the biting wind.

She punched in 911, put the phone to her ear and plunged into the shallowest part of the drift. By the third step, she was sinking in up to her thighs, and the snow quickly chilled her through the scrubs and long underwear she wore. When she lifted each foot, she scooped the icy crystals into her boots, where they melted, wetting her socks and freezing her skin.

The dispatch operator answered. "This is 911. What is the nature of your emergency?"

"I need to report a vehicle off in the ditch by... Oh, heck." Teresa glanced back up the hill. Since she'd been daydreaming, she had no idea how far she'd come or how close she was to reaching the nearest subdivision. "I'm somewhere along old Lee's Summit Road—between the medical center and 40 Highway. On the east side."

"Are you in the vehicle?"

"No, I just drove up on the accident." She broke through the snow at the bottom of the ditch and stepped into ankle-deep slush that soaked her to the skin in icy water. Her teeth chattered through the dispatcher's next question. "I'm sorry, what?"

"Is there anyone inside the truck?"

Teresa's wet feet left her shivering as she climbed out of the ditch. "Just a minute. Let me check."

She tilted her flashlight up to inspect the damaged vehicle. The driver's-side window was down—no, it was missing. It must have shattered with the impact of the crash, leaving tiny blunt shards along its bottom edge. Still, with the coming night and no light on inside the cab, she couldn't make out any driver or passenger. Not for the first time in her life, she silently cursed her diminutive height. When she reached the door of the jacked-up truck, she was too short to see in.

"Hello?" she called again. She reached up and tried the handle, but it was locked. She knocked on the door panel. "Is anyone in there?"

No response.

"Just a sec," she warned the dispatcher. Finding a safe spot to grasp the edge of the open window, she tucked the flashlight into her pocket, stepped onto the running board and pulled herself up. *"Madre de Dios."*

There was a man inside, slumped over the steering wheel. His dark blond hair was frosty with moisture. There was blood oozing from a knot on his forehead, and his skin was far too pale.

"Sir?" The ice cubes of her toes and the woman on the phone were forgotten as alarm, compassion and her years of training kicked in. "Sir?" She stuck the tip of her wool glove into her mouth and pulled it off with her teeth. She slipped two fingers beneath the collar of his padded leather jacket and pressed them to the side of his neck. Even with the thick jacket and the heater running, his skin was cold to the touch. But she could feel a pulse. It was faint and erratic, but it was there. "You're alive." She spat out the glove and raised her voice for the dispatcher to hear. "He's alive."

Pushing up onto her frozen toes, she gently leaned him back against the seat. With a groan, his head lolled toward his shoulder. A quick glance across the cab revealed a heavy nylon duffel bag but no other passenger to worry about.

"One victim," she reported. Hooking her arm inside the door to free her hands, she reached across his lap to turn off the ignition and saw more blood staining the front of his coat and the left leg of his jeans. "How fast were you going?" she mused out loud, wondering at the extent of his injuries. The wreck hadn't looked that bad from the road. Plus, he was still wearing his seat belt.

An answering moan silenced the random thoughts, and she moved her chilled fingers to his face, willing him to open his eyes. "Sir? Hey. I'm a nurse. I'm here to help." She pushed aside the damp spikes of straw-colored hair on his forehead to inspect the gash there. It might need a bandage, but no way could it account for all this blood. She pushed open one eyelid, then the other. Honey-brown irises looked back at her, trying to focus. She smiled. Good. Probably no concussion, then. "I need you to talk to me. I'm Teresa. What's your name?"

His pale lips drew together. "Don't need a candy striper, kid. Run along."

His speech was slurred. But it could be from the cold.

Kid? A little defensive fire crept into her veins before common sense reminded her to ignore the dig. The man was in trouble and needed her assistance. "I'm a registered nurse, and you're badly hurt. You want me to hike back to the road to get my hospital ID or do you want me to help?"

"Bossy little thing," he muttered. His eyes blinked open again, long enough to assess her face. "You're... nurse?"

"What's your name?" she repeated.

He inhaled a quick breath, gritted his teeth, then squeezed the words out. "Charles. I'm Charles."

"Like Charlie? Or Mr. Charles? No, don't close your eyes." She cupped her palm against the sandy beard stubble on his jaw. "Keep looking at me. Can you tell me where you're hurt?"

He pulled his left hand from his lap and grabbed the steering wheel. By sheer will, his vision seemed to sharpen and his gaze dropped to the phone tucked to her ear. "Is that 911?"

"Yes." When he reached for it, she handed it over. "Good idea. You can tell them exactly what hap— What are you doing? Give me my—"

"No cops." He disconnected the call and tossed her phone onto the dashboard. With a jerky shift of his broad shoulders, he pulled his right hand from beneath the duffel bag.

"¡Oh, mi Dios!"

He had a gun.

Teresa instinctively recoiled, but before she could jump off the running board, a big gloved hand anchored her arm to the door with surprising strength. "Let go!"

His fingers tightened around her wrist, trapping her

beside him as he pounded her phone with the butt of the wicked-looking pistol, smashing it into pieces.

"Hey!"

And then he turned the barrel of the gun on her. Bleeding Charles tilted his eyes up to the shoulder of the road. His voice was raspy, deep. "That your car, kid?"

Teresa's answer was a frozen gasp in the cold air. "Yes."

The gun barely wavered as he pushed open the door, forcing her into the snow. She landed on her butt and slid down the hill a few inches, but her bare hand, numb toes and panic slowed her efforts to scramble back onto her feet. He swung one long leg out, then the other, his black cowboy boots sinking into the snow, his breath hitching when his feet hit solid ground. Leaning against the cab for support, he pulled the duffel bag across the seat and tossed it at her. It hit her square in the stomach, knocking her onto her bottom again.

Judging by its weight and rattle, whatever was inside was heavy and metal and… "Son of a…" More guns.

Teresa shoved the bag away and climbed onto her knees, letting gravity pull her down into the ditch, farther away from the bleeding man, until she could find solid ground and bolt away.

She'd come to the aid of some drug dealer or gunrunner or mass murderer.

She was the one in trouble.

"I'd stop if I were you."

The ominous double click of a bullet sliding into the chamber of his automatic weapon rang clear in the crisp, frigid air, spurring her to her feet.

"I said stop!"

The deafening report of a gunshot froze her in her tracks. Teresa pushed her hood away from her face and turned her head, lifting her gaze to the tall, pale man with the narrowed eyes and bloody coat.

The mysterious Charles-slash-Mr. Charles was still leaning against the truck to hold himself up. But the gun he'd fired into the tree behind him was steaming in the cold air. The smell of sulfur filled her nose as he pulled the weapon down to aim it right at her. "Don't get any idea that you're going to run from me." His raspy, low-pitched threat was a whispery cloud in the night air. "Now you're going to pick up that bag and get me the hell out of here."

Chapter Three

Please don't make me scare you any worse than I have to, darlin', Nash silently begged. *Just do what I say. Take me where I want to go. And then you never have to deal with my sorry butt again.*

But those dark brown eyes tilting up to his were wide and frightened and telling him exactly what he didn't want to see—she was about to run.

"Ah, hell."

He was already sliding the gun into his holster when she spun around to leap across the bottom of the ditch. He was in no shape to chase anyone down, but she wasn't leaving him many options.

She landed on her hands and knees, a tangle of turquoise coat and pink scarf in the snow. But before she could find her footing, Nash ignored the protest jolting through his stiff leg and dove after her, using his six feet three inches of height to full advantage. He wasn't fast, but he was big enough to catch her around the thighs and tackle her. He landed across her legs and bottom, crushing her into the snow beneath him. Pain radiated through his shoulder as he hit the ground beside her, and he groaned.

But she didn't leave him any time to clench his teeth through the blinding agony or even to catch his breath.

With a feral roar, she rolled onto her back beneath him, spitting snow in his eyes and clawing at his neck and face.

"Get off me!"

Nash deflected the first blow. The second caught him square in the nose and made his eyes water. Hobbled by cold and pain and utter fatigue, he was about to be out-maneuvered by the thrashing woman unless he resorted to doing her some serious harm. And since he was still a hairbreadth away from that kind of desperation, he crawled on top of her and let his weight pin her down until the night stopped reeling about him.

She screamed in his ear and shoved a palmful of snow against his cheek.

"Stop struggling." The icy cold on his skin was like a reviving slap across the face. But when the empty fist arced toward him a second time, his temper flared. He caught her wrist with his good hand and pinned it on the ground above her head. "I said stop!"

For one surprising moment, she went still beneath him. Through the rapid puffs of breath that clouded the air between them, he took in the quick dart of her tongue across her full bottom lip and the halo of long coffee-brown hair fanning over the snow beneath her head. The defensive anger that had spiked inside him gave way to a flash of something wildly inappropriate for a wanted man fighting to survive for a few more days.

He was still processing those quick impressions of curves and heat and spirited beauty when she offered up a husky whisper. "What are you going to do with me?"

Keep your head in the game, Nash. Don't let the pretty girl distract you.

"Not a damn thing. Look, I don't want to be a part of your life any longer than you want to be a part of mine." Running on fumes, he summoned what little energy he had left and went the tough-guy route again. "You can either drive me where I want to go or I can take your keys. But I don't especially want to leave you abandoned out here on a night like this."

"Don't worry about me." He saw the spark in her eyes a split second before he felt her leg sliding beneath his and sensed her target.

Of all the... Nash pulled his knee between her thighs, beating her to the intimate contact. With a startled gasp, she went still again—long enough for him to release her wrists and unholster his gun. "I wouldn't if I were you."

"Those injuries aren't from any car wreck." Although her rosy cheeks indicated she was as aware of their intimate position as he was, it seemed nothing could silence that smart mouth. She brought her hands to the uninjured side of his chest, and he let her shove a few inches of breathing room between them. "And that's body armor. Who are you, Mr. Charles? What did you do?"

"The less you know about me, the better." Good. He hadn't slipped and given her his name in his groggy state in the truck. That meant it wasn't out there on the wire or in cyberspace, flagging his location to the cartel or the inside man who'd set him up.

Nash raised his head and glanced around him, suddenly wary that he'd already spent too long out in the open. That gunshot he'd used to intimidate her when he realized he couldn't stop her from running might have alerted a nearby farmer or some other fool who was out here in the middle of nowhere on this wintry night. And even though he'd severed her call, the authorities were almost certainly already on their way.

He assessed the subdued flight risk in her warm chocolate eyes before easing his hips off hers and gingerly pushing himself up on one knee in the snow. "I don't have much time. I can't afford to let the police get here before I'm gone—and you're my only way out of here, Peewee. I need you to grab my bag and get me to your car, then take me someplace where you can patch me up."

"Peewee?" She sat up as soon as she was free. A second later she was scooting away, climbing to her feet and brushing the snow off the clinging wet cotton of her pink pant legs. "I should just leave you here to freeze to death."

"Can you outrun a bullet?" If she tried, he'd have to let her go. But he was hoping he still had that big-and-mean-and-on-his-last-nerve look going for him to convince her to cooperate.

Apparently, he did.

Although that defiant spark never left her dark eyes, she lifted her gaze from the gun up to his, nodding her acquiescence. "Now that you've conveniently gotten us both soaked to the skin, we're at risk for hypothermia if we stay out here much longer. And I'm not dying for the likes of you."

She stumbled down the hill, kicking her way through knee-deep snow with every step. Man, she was a little spitfire. Maybe not as afraid of him as she should be, and definitely not the teenager he'd first thought her to be. She stood over his go bag, breathing deeply, rubbing her bare hand inside her gloved one, no doubt feeling the cold and damp, especially after that tumble in the snow.

Or maybe she was contemplating another avenue of escape.

Nash shifted the angle of the gun toward her. "Pick it up and don't try to run again," he warned. With an answering glare, she hoisted the heavy bag onto her shoulder. It was almost as big as she was. But other than a Spanish curse beneath her breath, she trudged up the hill without further protest or complaint.

Nash, however, struggled to find his footing. His leg ached but felt solid enough. It was more a case of finding his balance and catching his breath. He lurched to his feet, swaying with the first step. White spots swam before his eyes, but it was more than the snow swirling past.

The nurse was several steps ahead of him when she dropped the bag into a drift at the shoulder of the road and turned.

Nash willed the light-headedness to go away and raised the gun toward her. But his left arm hung at his side and his right was getting weaker. "I said—"

"I don't think I can carry you both," she groused, marching back down the hill.

He almost laughed at the idea of this little bundle of sass thinking she was going to carry him. But she moved to his right side, wound her arm behind his waist and urged him to put his arm around her shoulders. "Lean on me," she ordered.

Nash hesitated. She fit right beneath his arm, the perfect height for the crutch he apparently needed. And yeah, it put the crown of that silky dark hair that had fallen out of its ponytail and gotten dotted with snow right beneath his chin. He tightened his grip around the gun that rested on her shoulder when she grabbed his wrist and butted her hip up against his. Was this cozying-up tactic some kind of trick to get the weapon away from him?

"Come on, tough guy." She latched her fingers around his belt and tugged. "You can get fresh with me in the snow and threaten me with a gun all you want. But if you really want my help, you'll put your weight on me and move your feet." She flashed her dark eyes up to him before urging him forward with a jerk at his waist and a grunt of effort. "In about two minutes, my extremities are going to be so numb I won't be able to do anything for either of us—even if you do shoot. So move."

He couldn't have been rescued by some meek, mousy thing who'd do what he said without the attitude? He tapped the butt of the gun against her shoulder. "That's pretty bold talk for a woman who's got no advantage."

"Uh-huh. I'm not the one bleeding to death. Your color's awful. Your skin is cold to the touch. I don't want your dead body on my conscience." She tugged again, forcing him to take a step. "How long have you been losing blood?"

"The leg's just a graze," he informed her, bracing more of his weight on her shoulders to limp another step up the hill. "I stanched the hole in my chest," he ground out as his right boot slipped and he came down hard on his injured leg.

"Nice dodge," she chided. "That means longer than you want to admit." She yanked back on his belt to keep him from falling. "So if you won't tell me about your injuries, then tell me what the other guy looks like."

The exertion of climbing the hill and keeping his wits about him left Nash gasping for breath. But he kept moving. "You don't want to know."

Three steps. Four. They'd reached the tracks in the snow where he'd plowed through the drift on the shoulder of the road. "Is he kidnapping some poor unlucky Good Samaritan, too?"

"Nope. They aren't doing anything right now."

"They?" She was breathing as hard as he was when she stopped beside the car and tipped her face up to his. "Wait a minute. Are they…? Did you…?"

"Yeah, darlin'. I killed all three of them."

"Killed—?"

"I preferred them in the morgue instead of me."

Her cheeks blanched as she opened the passenger door. "You murdered three men?"

No jury would call what he'd done anything but self-defense. But she didn't have to know that those hired guns had come to the warehouse to murder *him*. And Tommy. Remembering the young man dead on the warehouse floor created a different kind of pain in Nash's chest. He should have dragged the body to his truck, made sure Agent Delvecchio got the proper burial he deserved, instead of letting him lie alongside his own killers on a cold concrete floor. Losing Tommy had been like losing a kid brother. One by one, Graciela and his thugs were taking out the closest thing he had to family. There had to be justice. They had to pay.

Nah. He wouldn't feel remorse about taking advantage of this woman's nursing skills or scaring her into the no-questions-asked cooperation he needed. Even if he wound up dead at the end of all this, he was going to make sure the traitor was exposed and no one else on his team died.

"You gonna stop giving me trouble now, Peewee?" He looked down at her and saw the bravado or anger or whatever had fueled her defiance these past few minutes disappear. Now she was finally truly afraid of him. Ignoring a deep stab of guilt and reminding himself of the necessity for haste and maintaining anonymity—for her sake as well as his—he lowered himself into the seat of her midsize car. He pointed the gun over the crest of the hill. "Now the bag. Put it in the back."

With a nod, she hurried to obey his orders. Fisting the gun in his lap, Nash risked tipping his head back against the headrest and closing his eyes for a few seconds. The heat inside the car was a drugging mix of pain and relief. The thawing nerve endings around his wounds and frozen toes stung like hundreds of needles piercing his skin. Yet drawing warm air into his lungs after so many hours exposed to the elements seemed to ease the constriction in his chest. Maybe it was the influx of oxygen into his system, or maybe these were the last moments of his life seeping away, and all he wanted to do was sleep.

This was humiliating, to be so helpless, so dependent on a frightened woman for survival. And while he might be more comfortable giving orders to his men or smacktalking his way with the bad guys, he'd sweet-talked a woman or two in his day. But that required a degree of thought and patience, and minding the words that came out of his mouth, that he didn't possess the energy to stay on top of this evening. So he'd resorted to the bull-in-a-china-shop approach to gaining her cooperation.

Once he was in better shape, he'd let her go. She could report him to the local police after she'd gotten him off this exposed stretch of road, stitched him up and bought him a few hours of rest. Of course, by the time he released her and any cops got wind of his presence here in Kansas City, he intended to be long gone.

The car door slammed behind him, startling him from a dozing state, reminding him that he probably needed a good twelve hours of rest and recovery time before he could let his reluctant rescuer contact anyone. That meant he had to stay alert and he had to stay mean to maintain the upper hand and keep her from asking any questions or turning him in. If she never found out who he was or who was after him, the cartel wouldn't be able to tie him to her. He needed her to believe he was a threat, but Nash intended to walk away without doing more than inconveniencing her for one night. Berto Graciela and Santiago Vargas and their selfish greed were real dangers he wouldn't risk her life on by making her any kind of witness or information source.

When she opened the driver's door and got in, the blast of cold air revived him further. "Let's go."

Instead of obeying, she cranked the heat, peeled off her remaining glove and rubbed her fingers in front of the heating vent. He could see her visibly shaking now, but he wondered how much of that was the cold and how much was fear. "What's going to happen to me?"

"Nothing, if you do what I tell you."

She slid him a sideways glance before focusing on bringing warmth back to her fingers again. "You owe me a new phone."

The corner of his mouth wanted to crook with amusement at the woman's refusal to say die. Ignoring his growing admiration for her spirit, though, he reached over and turned the heat back down to low—partly to keep his head clear and partly to remind her who was in charge. "Drive."

"I'd like to wait until I can feel my toes first."

He shifted the gun in his lap. "It wasn't a request."

She tucked a long strand of tangled hair behind her ear, peeking at him around her hand. Her gaze dropped to the Smith & Wesson pointed at her before she buckled herself in and shifted the car into gear. "You're a bully, you know that?"

"I know," he answered, surprised she hadn't called him worse. Nash checked the mirrors right along with her, ensuring the road was clear in both directions before she pulled out. "Did you give 911 my license plate number?"

"No. I was more worried about your safety. Stupid me, huh?"

Good. That should buy them a few minutes. A police officer, ambulance and fire engine were most likely already en route to the scene. But if she hadn't reported his truck, then the authorities wouldn't be able to track him or put his name over the wires until they arrived on site. And he intended to be long gone by then.

She tapped on the brake, slowing their speed as they neared the bottom of the hill. "What are you, a hit man? Drug dealer? Is that what's in that bag? Your payoff? Drugs and guns? Is there some innocent man somewhere I should have stopped to help instead of you?"

"Less talking, more driving."

She nudged on the accelerator as they followed the dark ribbon of road up the next hill. "The moisture in the air is freezing on the pavement, so I don't trust myself to turn around here. I'll have to drive up to the next intersection or driveway to turn around and get you back to the med center."

"We're not going to the hospital."

"Then where…?" She stomped on the brakes and they started to skid.

His instinctive reaction to reach for the wheel burned through his shoulder like a fresh gunshot. Nash swore as the edge of the road zoomed up to his window.

But she jerked the wheels into the skid, jerked them the other way. Leaving dirt and drift on the blacktop behind them, she steered them back to the middle of the road.

"Easy, Peewee." Nash gritted his teeth as new waves of pain shot through him. "We need to get there in one piece."

She slowed their speed and guided them back into the right lane. "Enough with the nicknames, okay?"

He nudged back the front of his jacket and pulled the blood-soaked bandanna from beneath his vest. His time was already limited—he didn't need a panicked driver cutting it any shorter. "I thought you were a kid when you first walked up to my truck. What are you? Five foot nothin'?"

"I'm five-three. I'm not even the shortest one in my family, and I'm not going to have any personal conversation with you." She glanced over at the bandanna dripping on his pant leg. "Here." She released her death grip on the steering wheel to untie the pink scarf from her neck and pull it free. She tossed it across the seat into his lap. "Pack that against the wound. The cold temps have probably slowed the bleeding enough for you to survive this long. You need to see a doctor."

"I've got a nurse."

"A pediatric nurse," she reminded him.

Bit by bit, he stuffed the scarf beneath his vest. "Can you stitch up a wound?"

"Yes, but you need antibiotics. Maybe even surgery. At the very least, you need an X-ray to find out what damage that bullet's done inside you."

"I'm not going to any damn hospital."

"Then where am I taking you? The nearest cemetery?"

"That's a sweet bedside manner you've got there, darlin'." She reached over and shut off the heat. "Turn it back on. You're shivering."

"Like you care." She shook her head. "The cold's better for you. That's probably the only reason why you haven't bled to death yet."

"You're a smart girl."

"I'm not a *girl*." She said the word as if it left a sour taste in her mouth.

"No, you're not." Her cute little curvy shape and endless backbone proved that. Her grown-up strength was also giving him an idea for plan B or C or whatever letter of the alphabet he was on now with this mess of an assignment. He could see the glow of lights in the distance now, a neighborhood or highway interchange, he guessed. But there was still no oncoming traffic or vehicles on the road behind them. The site of his crash had been swallowed up by hills and darkness. So the ambulance and cops must be coming from the south—not the direction they were headed. He'd have to play the kidnapper for a day or so longer, but he could make this work. "You married?"

"No."

"Got a boyfriend? Kids? Roommate?"

She smiled, but there was no humor in her tone. "I've got a big brother who's a cop. A fugitive like you is probably already on his radar."

Good. "So no boyfriend, either."

"I didn't say—"

"Eyes on the road," he warned when she glared at him again. "You don't play the big-brother card unless you've got no other man in your life to stick up for you. You live alone."

Her fists tightened around the steering wheel. "My personal life is none of your business."

This plan was going to work. The woman lived alone and no one was expecting her. She had the skills he needed—if he could just keep her in line. "A pretty little thing like you with that sassy mouth and no husband or boyfriend? Are you a widow or a workaholic?"

"Am I a...?" He met her glare this time, and she quickly glanced away. "It's...complicated."

As intriguing as that answer might be to follow up on, Nash had the information he needed. She lived alone. No one was expecting her for a date. No one would worry if she didn't check in for the next few hours. Steer clear of the cop big brother—if he wasn't just a story she'd made up to try to intimidate him—and this plan could work. "Trust me. I understand complicated."

"I bet you do." They passed a sign indicating a state highway up ahead. She pointed to the traffic lights in the distance. "Am I taking you to your place? Just tell me where to turn. I'm bad with street names. I promise if I see the address, I'll erase it right out of my head."

"I'm not from here."

"Are we going to your hideout?"

"Hideout?" Amusement threatened a smile again. "Isn't that a little Sam Spade-ish?"

"Whatever you call it. To meet up with your friends? Will they take care of you? Or are they the three men who did that to you?"

"They were from…" Ah, hell. He was saying too much. He didn't want to give her any names or places she might share later. "I don't have friends in K.C."

"Why doesn't that surprise me?" She adjusted her lights down from bright as a car coming from the opposite direction appeared over the next hill. "Why *are* you here?"

"You ask an awful lot of questions, darlin'."

"Darlin'? I think I prefer Peewee."

Nash considered her answer. He could give a little as long as she was cooperating. "What's your name again?"

"Teresa." She rolled her *R* with a musical lilt.

"Take me home, Teresa."

"You said you weren't from here." Her gaze darted down to the dashboard, and her posture straightened a tiny bit, putting him on guard. "Oh. I wondered where the twang of yours was from. How far south are we going? I'll need to stop for gas if we're driving any distance. There are a couple of gas stations up on 40 Highway."

Really? She thought she could outfox him and stop in

a public place where she could call for help? His momentary lapse into nice-guy territory had just ended. "Don't get too smart, Teresa." He nodded toward the needle on her dash before raising his gun in his lap. "Your tank is practically full. Very responsible for this kind of weather. Nice try, though. I'm guessing our destination isn't that far or you wouldn't be on this backwater stretch of road. You're taking me to *your* place."

Chapter Four

How had this happened to her?

How had she gone off on such a wrong turn from proving herself to be a smart, self-sufficient adult? She'd been taken hostage by a bleeding stranger, and now she was helping him limp up the steps into her apartment building—sneaking a fugitive into her own home! Although he carried her bag of groceries in the hand at the end of his injured arm, and they walked hip to hip as if they enjoyed holding on to each other, there was nothing normal about this stroll from the parking lot.

Teresa felt the barrel of Mr. Charles's gun nudge her side through the blanket she'd draped around his shoulders to mask his weapon and injuries from anyone who might see them stumbling across the scraped and salted concrete. "Remember," he warned in that deep-pitched drawl of his, "if anyone asks, we just took a tumble in the snow. You say anything to anyone that gives me away, and this bullet will go right through that pretty hide of yours."

Maybe *Gamberro was* her middle name, and her older brother and sisters were right to worry about her.

"I get it. You have a gun. I'll do what you say." She hiked that mysterious black bag of his higher onto her shoulder, freeing her arm to unlock the outer door. She had to release her grip on the back of his belt to hold it open for him.

But there was no thought of closing the door behind him and running away. The man was like a wounded bear. Even without the gun, her captor was mean and unpredictable and all sinewy brawn. Although he said he wanted to draw as little attention to himself as possible, she had no doubt he'd shoot right through the glass or wrestle her to the ground again if she didn't do his bidding.

"This is crazy," she whispered, sliding her arm behind his back again, steadying his uneven gait. "You're going to die. And I don't want a dead man in my apartment."

"Then don't let me die."

There were two more stairs inside before they reached the carpeted lobby and elevators. The fist of fear squeezing her gut tightened with every step. What would he do if she couldn't make him well enough to travel? Who was he running from? Were there other armed men in the city looking for him? What if she was still his prisoner when they found him? The sooner she could send him on his way and call her brother, AJ, to report him, the better. "We should have gone to the hospital."

"Not an option."

"You'd rather die than be turned over to the police?" Teresa pushed the call button and the doors opened. "What if I can't fix you? I don't exactly have a fully equipped E.R. in my apartment."

He limped in beside her and rested his backside against the railing, easing some of his weight off her shoulders. "A smart girl like you will figure it out. What floor?"

"I'm in 417." Teresa pushed the number 4. "What if you die? Is there someone worse than you out there who's going to blame me?"

"No one cares if I die. Only if I live."

Teresa swung her gaze up to the haggard shadows darkening his eyes. "I don't care what you've done—that's a horrible thing to say."

As the doors started to close, a familiar quavering voice called out from the lobby. "Hold the door, please. My arms are full."

"Don't you dare, dar—"

But Teresa had already pushed the door-open button. She wasn't sure if it was ingrained politeness or some latent survival instinct kicking in that made her ignore his warning and invite company into the elevator with them. Florence Walker, with her snow-white hair pulled up in a bun on top of her head, toddled into the elevator car with a basket of neatly folded clothes perched on her hip. "Good evening, Teresa. I'm trying to be healthy and use the stairs to do my laundry, especially since I can't get out and walk now. But my knee only made it up one flight from the basement before I decided exercise is for the birds."

"Good evening, Mrs. Walker. This cold weather will aggravate your arthritis."

Those same light brown eyes that had been matter-of-factly devoid of emotion a moment earlier drilled her with a silent warning. He straightened beside her, keeping his long thigh—and the gun—in contact with her body.

But the woman who lived in the apartment beneath Teresa's seemed completely unaware of any tension inside the elevator. She glanced up at the man wearing a blanket draped around him like a serape and smiled at Teresa. "Am I interrupting something? A date?"

A date? Florence thought *this* was the kind of man Teresa wanted in her life?

The elevator bobbed once before it slowly began to

rise. The motion rocked Teresa into her captor's side. He slid his arm behind her and let the icy steel of his gun rest on the curve of her bottom. She flinched at another round of full-body contact with his tall, hard frame.

And flinched again when she realized she hadn't immediately pushed some space between them. How sick. Why would she even notice the shape of his body? Was her skin tingling with awareness at being pressed against him? No, it had to be the numbing cold wearing off now that they were inside. She should not—could not—think that there was anything to like about this dangerous bully of a man.

Trouble. Trouble. Trouble.

"Have I embarrassed you, dear? Your cheeks are red."

Teresa tore herself from her humiliating thoughts to look into the concerned blue eyes behind Florence's wire-rimmed glasses. "No. Of course not. I… It's the cold."

Flattening her palm against the worn wool of the blanket, she tried to put some distance between them. If anything, he moved closer, pushing his rib cage against her hand and wedging her firmly against the gun at her back. She needed to get away from this man. Now. But how? Running hadn't worked. Neither had arguing or begging.

Her gaze fell to the drops of blood on her captor's round-toed boot. *Look, Mrs. Walker. Be suspicious. Help me.* Teresa lifted her gaze to Florence, willing the older woman to notice the danger she was in, silently asking her to go to her apartment and dial 911. "Mr., um…" *See? If this was a date, wouldn't I know his name?* Teresa made sure her smile looked forced. "This, um, man I just met is feeling a little under the weather." She glanced down at the tiny bloodstains again. *Look.* "He—"

"I took a nasty fall and got hurt." Florence might not

be noticing the clues Teresa was giving her, but her captor certainly had. "Might have dislocated my shoulder."

"Oh, I'm sorry to hear that." Florence clucked her tongue against her teeth. "You really have to watch that ice."

Really? This sweet, clueless woman was sympathizing with the ratty, pale stranger instead of the neighbor who lived in the apartment above her and shared tea on the fire escape when the weather was nice? Teresa bit down on her frustration and tried communicating a silent cry for help one more time. "I offered to drive him to the hospital, but—"

"She's taking real good care of me, ma'am." He grinned and lifted the bag of groceries he held a few shaky inches. "She's going to fix me a nice hot meal."

Florence turned her full attention up to Mr. Charles. No way would she notice the blood now. "I imagine our Teresa would make any patient of hers feel better. She's the sweetest young lady in our whole building."

"I bet you give her a run for her money." Was he flirting with the older woman?

Mrs. Walker laughed. "Now, aren't you a dear." She winked at Teresa, without noticing one bit of distress. "This one's a keeper. Not only is he tall and good-looking in that scruffy cowboy kind of way, but he's a charmer."

A keeper? Charming? *Do you see me smiling?* "I'm just his nurse. He's a patient."

"If that's what you want to call it." The elevator dinged for Mrs. Walker's floor and slowed its ascent. Florence winked at Teresa and smiled. "Don't you worry. I may be old, but I read books. I know what codespeak is. I won't tell your family that you had a young man over tonight."

That was what she thought all the pleading signals had been about? Hiding a lover from her family?

The elevator doors opened, and Florence headed down the hallway.

"Mrs. Walker? Would you—?" But a poke of steel against Teresa's hip stopped her from calling back her white-haired neighbor.

The older woman turned. "Yes, dear?"

Her captor dropped his head, his breath a warm tickle against her ear. "Give me away and I'll shoot *her*."

Teresa tilted her head back to read the deadly promise in his honey-brown eyes.

Somehow, she remembered how to smile when she spoke to Florence Walker again. "Thanks for keeping my secret."

"Of course, dear. You two have fun playing doctor."

Mr. Charles reached behind Teresa to tap the door-close button with the end of his gun. "Good night, ma'am."

"Good night."

The moment the doors drifted shut, Teresa pushed him away, hating that little sting of guilt she felt when he grunted with the effort to keep himself on his feet. "Really? You'd shoot that sweet old grandmother?"

"Whatever it takes to survive." He sagged back against the railing, his jaw clenched in a tight cord of pain. "You don't have to like me, Peewee. You just have to do what I tell you."

"I hate you," she muttered into the corner.

"That's the idea." Whatever injuries he'd sustained, his hearing was just fine. The elevator had barely started to move before the bell dinged again. "We're here. Fourth floor, right?"

For a split second, Teresa considered bolting out of the elevator and letting the doors trap the slow-moving man behind her. But the last thing she wanted was for Mrs.

Walker or any of the other innocent residents to stumble onto a collapsed gunman in the elevator, think they were doing the right thing by stopping to help him and end up his prisoner. At least she had some understanding of how the criminal mind worked. With a murdered father, a brother who was a cop and a sister who worked in the E.R., she stood a better chance of getting out of this unscathed than any of the elderly residents or young families who lived in the apartment building with her.

"Come on." She braced her wet boot against the door when it started to slide shut and reached for the wounded man. "Let's get you inside before you threaten any other neighbors."

He tossed his right arm around her shoulders, leaning on her a little more heavily than before as he stepped out beside her. "You always this mouthy, Peewee?"

"Pretty much."

The chuckle that rumbled in his throat became a groan of pain. He was in bad shape, probably even worse than he'd let on. As much as she normally admired that kind of determination to survive in a patient, a part of her wished he'd go ahead and pass out so that she could take his gun and escape to call AJ and the police. She had to lean him against the wall beside her door and drop the deadly black bag so she could fish out her keys from her purse. By the time she had the knob and dead bolt open, he'd dropped the sack of groceries to the floor beside his boot. The blanket he wore had gaped open to reveal the bloody shoulder of his jacket and the gun down at his side. His face was pale and his eyes had drifted shut.

"Don't you die here," she warned, as concern mixed with anger, fear and the impulse to run from the dangerous man.

"Not yet, darlin'. Not yet." Those golden-brown eyes

opened, looking straight down at her. He shifted the gun to his weak hand and swiped the ring of keys from her fingers before pushing his way inside the door ahead of her. "Grab the food and my bag."

Damn it. She hated feeling any kind of compassion for this man even more than she hated being forced to help him. She should have run when she'd had the chance.

Dropping his belongings on the tiled entryway without any regard for the bag's noisy contents was the only protest she made when he locked the door behind her. He slipped her keys into the pocket of his jeans while she took off her wet coat and draped it over the back of a dining-room chair, then carried the smushed groceries to the kitchen peninsula.

"What is this? Santa's workshop?"

Teresa turned and eyed the rolls of wrapping paper, ribbon and sacks of yet-to-be-wrapped presents strewn across the top of the table. "I have a big family with lots of nieces and nephews. Don't bad guys celebrate Christmas, too?"

"Not this year." She caught his gaze across the entryway and thought she detected something more like longing in his weary gaze, rather than the sarcasm she'd imagined in his tone.

But when his eyes focused and met her curious perusal, his expression hardened like ice. He limped up beside her at the kitchen peninsula, reaching over to the phone above the counter and pulling out the line that connected it to the wall jack. "Hey!"

"My rules, darlin'." That cord ended up in the pocket with her keys as he scanned the main rooms of her apartment, no doubt looking for any other means of communication to disable. When his gaze landed on her again, the bully who gave the orders was back. "Pull that table over in front of the door."

"You have the gun, remember? I'm not running."

"Forgive me if I don't trust you."

With a huff, Teresa scooted the chair aside and lifted the edge of the oak table she'd inherited from her mother.

"Wait." Before she'd dragged it a foot, he was waving her away from the table with the gun and pointing into the living room. "Try the sofa." Again, as soon as she started sliding it across the carpet, he stopped her. He nodded to the armoire against the wall where her television and sound system were stored. "Can you move that?"

A tad breathless, Teresa straightened, shoving her long, damp hair off her face. "Not unless I empty it out first."

"Good."

"What are you...?" As she curled her cold toes inside her boots to curb the urge to stop him, he put his good shoulder to the thick oak wood and pushed it in front of the door, effectively barricading the exit.

"Like I said, I don't...trust..." He was bent over, breathing heavily, the fist with the gun braced on one knee, by the time he was finished. The man was running on fumes and sheer determination. But even that massive stubborn streak wouldn't sustain him much longer.

"You really have a death wish, don't you. You'd better sit before you keel over." She picked up the blanket that had fallen to the floor and hooked her hand beneath his elbow, guiding him over to a stool at the kitchen peninsula. She draped the blanket over his head and shoulders, futilely trying to ignore the way, even when he was sitting down, that he was still a head taller than she was. It was equally hard not to notice how his chest and shoulders were broad and muscled and seriously imposing up close like this. She didn't need the gun in his lap or the nothing-to-lose expression in his eyes to know she was completely at his mercy. She tucked the tattered edges of the blanket together and quietly pulled away. "Try to stay warm while I get my things."

Instead of obeying even that most practical suggestion, he sloughed the blanket to the floor and stumbled after her into the bathroom, where she fetched her first-aid kit. His ragged breathing stirred the crown of her hair as he trailed her to the linen closet, too, where she pulled out her sewing kit and a stack of towels and washcloths.

But when she would have returned to the kitchen, he raised the gun and forced her on into the bedroom at the end of the hall. He spotted the phone on her bedside table and disconnected its cord just as he had the one in the kitchen. "You can work in here."

"In my bedroom?" What kind of sick twist was he adding to this abduction-and-intimidation game now? "Look, I don't know what else you think you can threaten me with, but I won't let you touch—"

"Don't flatter yourself, Peewee. In another lifetime, I might be tempted by all those curves. But tonight I only need you to be my nur...se." He swore at the strain of shoving her bed in front of the window and the snow-packed fire escape outside. He collapsed onto the edge of the mattress, cradling his wounded arm in his lap. His rugged face was pale as a ghost, his lips quivering and nostrils flaring as he struggled to catch his breath. With another vicious curse, he tugged his ruined jacket off his shoulder, slowly uncovering the flak vest and her blood-soaked scarf sticking out from the neck and arm-hole. "The only other point of entry to your apartment is in here. And you'll have to get past me to get out."

If it hadn't been for the gun clutched in his fist, she'd

have banked on him passing out and would have climbed right over him without batting an eye to open that window and hurry down to Mrs. Walker's to use her phone. But the one thing on the man that didn't seem to be affected by his injuries was his grip on that gun. And, as intent as he was on ripping open the vest's Velcro straps beneath each arm, she believed his assertion that using her bed as an examination table was only about keeping her prisoner, nothing more. So she set her supplies on the bed beside him, pulled on a pair of sterile gloves from the first-aid kit and went to work.

"Here, Mr. Charles. Let me." She took over getting the jacket and protective vest off him, dumping both on the rug at her feet. She touched his right arm, pushing his hand up to the scarf, avoiding the gun while asking for his help. "Keep pressure on the wound."

"It's just Charles," he answered, pressing the wool against his shoulder. "Charlie, to some."

She pulled a pair of scissors from her sewing basket. "Do you have a last name, Charles?"

"Be careful with those." She was keenly aware of his eyes following her every move as she cut away the left side of his black knit shirt and T-shirt. "You get any idea about stabbing me and I'll—"

"So no last name?" She carefully peeled away the bloodied layers of cotton, exposing a landscape of corded muscle, dark bruises and faint white scars dotting his skin. "*Madre de Dios.* What happened to you?"

"Had a disagreement with three guys who wanted to kill me, wrecked my truck, tussled with a petite brunette in the snow."

"Stop it." Compassion fisted in her gut as she touched her gloved fingertip to the oldest and palest mark branding his biceps, tracing the puckered ring, raising goose bumps across his ashy skin. "This is from an old gun-shot wound. My brother has a scar like this. The kind of work you do must take a terrible toll on your body. And yet you keep going back for more punishment. Who did this to you? Who's after you?"

"You feeling sorry for me, Peewee?" He turned his face to hers, the low rumble of his voice whispering across her skin like a warm breeze.

"You've been hurt so many..." Her voice trailed away when she realized how close she was standing to him. Her fingers still rested against his arm. Her thighs were touching his. And if she angled her head a fraction to the left, her cheek would slide against the raspy stubble of his jaw. Her heart rate kicked up a notch, thundering in her ears. Those firm male lips were just a hair-breadth away from the apple of her cheek. Seriously? She couldn't catch her breath? She was turned on by this brute? Surprise and shame poured through her blood, and she pulled her hand away, retreating a step from his disturbing masculine heat.

What was happening to her? She must be suffering from some form of Stockholm syndrome already, feeling this perverted connection to her captor. She hated this man for threatening her life, for endangering Florence Walker and the rest of her neighbors simply by being here. He'd taken advantage of her desire to help some-one in need and made her feel like a fool for doing so. He'd made her angry and afraid. She couldn't feel sorry for the terrible harm that had been done to him over the years, and she certainly wasn't attracted to him.

Yes, the men her sisters usually set her up with were safe and boring. None of the men she'd dated had ever made her heart thump against her ribs with an irrational awareness like this. This reaction to Charles No-Name

Mystery Man was just fear talking. Adrenaline. These unwanted feelings of compassion and attraction to the hard planes of his body and the soft color of his eyes didn't mean she had a death wish to get involved with anyone as dangerous and controlling as this creep.

She picked up a washcloth. "No. You made the choice to do what you do. If you want to lead a life of violence, I suppose it makes sense that you'd bear the marks of that decision."

But when she turned around to walk to the bathroom sink to wet the cloth, Charles clamped a hand around her wrist like a vise, pulling her back between his knees. "You don't have to understand me at all, Teresa." Her gaze dropped to the gun on the quilt beside him, and he quickly released her to snatch it up before she could even think about making a lunge for it. "I'm not going to tell you my last name, because the less you know about me, the better. You may not believe this, but I'm trying to protect you."

She retreated beyond his reach, rubbing at the traitorous warmth that lingered on her skin where he'd touched her. "Hence the threats and the kidnapping."

"Does that mouth ever get you into trouble? Or is all the tough talk just a defense mechanism for you?" He nodded, as if something in her posture or expression had answered his question. "Try not to be too afraid. If you do everything I say, you'll be safe."

Teresa was too wet and cold and exhausted to stifle her sarcasm. "Well, guess what, Charlie. I don't trust you, either."

The corner of his mouth crooked up with half a grin at her expense. "No wonder you don't have a boyfriend. You're prickly when you get worried or riled up."

"I'm not worried about you," she lied.

The grin faded as he tugged at the scarf, now sticky with his blood, exposing the ragged wound at the front of his shoulder. "The people who tried to kill me this morning will try again. They've already tracked me to Kansas City. I have no doubt they'll send someone else to find me and finish the job. I don't want you caught in the crossfire. Enough innocent lives have already been lost."

"What do you care about innocent lives?"

"Even men like me have a code of honor they live by. Rules about what's right and wrong." There was no trace of humor anywhere in his expression now. With the flecks of gold-and-brown beard dotting his neck and jaw, he looked even more like the wounded bear she'd imagined him to be earlier. He dropped the scarf onto the other soiled garments on the floor and raised his gaze to hers. "Rule One? I need to live. For a few days longer, at least. To do that, I need your help. That makes you an asset to me. Rule Two is protect your assets. So no last name. No warm fuzzies between us. I don't need you to get close or to give a damn about me. Just do your job."

"In a few days, it'll be Christmas," she pointed out. "Is there really a rule on that list of yours that says you're going to let me go once I take out that bullet?" He arched a wheat-colored brow in a silent question. She moved around his knees and pointed to the bump in the skin beside his scapula. "I can see it protruding through the skin near your shoulder blade. Your protective vest must have worked in reverse. Instead of keeping the bullet out, it prevented the projectile from exiting your body. You need a surgeon, not a pediatric nurse."

He shook his head. "I've got you. That's all I need."

"You're lucky it's not buried inside by a lung or other vital organ. And there's no way to tell what muscle or bone damage there is without an X-ray." She didn't bother reminding him again that a hospital was where they should be right now.

He tipped that grizzled bear of a face up to hers. "Can you cut it out and stitch up the wound?"

Did he not understand the enormity of what he was asking of her? "Yes, but that's only a superficial fix. A muscle tear will probably heal on its own. But if there's a bone chip inside or a nicked blood vessel or nerve damage—"

"Do it."

"I need a few minutes to boil water and sterilize everything."

"No boiling water." He slipped his long arm behind her waist, pulling her close again. "You think I'm going to trust you with a potential weapon like that?"

Ignoring the heavy weight of the weapon resting against her hip, Teresa jerked away. "You may have no problem hurting people, but it's not my job or my nature to intentionally inflict any harm."

"Oh, yeah? Who was going to knee me a half hour ago?"

Guilty. She silently thanked him for the reminder she needed to clear her head of her confusing feelings. "I've got isopropyl alcohol in the bathroom." She thumbed over her shoulder to the hallway. "Is it all right if I go and get that?"

Charles the Bully simply nodded.

She returned with a bowl of soapy water and a bottle of rubbing alcohol and went to work cleaning and sterilizing as much of the wound, needle, thread and paring knife she'd brought from the kitchen as she could. At his bidding, she'd turned her dresser mirror so that he could watch her work with the knife behind him. It was the reflection of jaded suspicion she spoke to now. "This isn't standard procedure. And these conditions are far from sterile. What if I make it worse?"

His gaze met hers in the mirror. "Trust me, darlin', I'm as tough as I look. You can't make me hurt any worse than I already do."

"The sooner you're fixed up, the sooner you're out of my life, right? Even though I know your name and can describe your face, I'll be a free woman again? You won't hurt anyone else?"

Those golden eyes, seemingly lit from within, offered her an unexpected reassurance. "You're not who I'm after, darlin'. You're not the one who needs to worry about me."

So who was he after? Who should be worried about the toughness and the single-minded determination and all the guns she suspected were in that bag? Charles was big, strong, wounded, armed and serious as a heart attack. Whoever he was after *should* be afraid. She'd been a fool for not minding her tongue and risking his anger, for thinking for even one minute that she could run away or leave him behind or talk him into letting her go before he was done with her.

Shivering again, though with something more unsettling than the cold of her damp clothes, Teresa dropped her gaze to the broad expanse of his back. She opened the antiseptic spray and doused the injured shoulder. "This is only a topical anesthetic. When I cut through the skin, it's going to hurt. If you cry out, the neighbors will hear. I don't want anyone calling 911 and getting caught in the middle of another shoot-out with you."

"I won't cry out."

She didn't know whether to admire or fear a man with that kind of control. In the end, she reminded herself that what she felt didn't matter. As a nurse, she simply did her job and took care of the patient, no matter what it might cost her emotionally.

Teresa patched him up the best she could. She cleaned and bandaged the wound on his left thigh, as well. An hour later, she had an exhausted man, dressed in little more than gauze and tape and the fresh jeans he'd pulled from that bag, sitting on the edge of her bed. He was flexing the fingers of his left hand. Although it still pained him to raise his arm, he was getting some feeling and use back in the hand, making him twice as dangerous as the one-armed thug had been. Per his instructions, she dumped the ruined clothing and medical supplies into a trash bag and picked it up to carry it out to the kitchen to dispose of later.

"You got any duct tape, Peewee?" he asked, slowly pushing to his feet. He towered over her, even in his bare feet, reminding her who was in charge. Teresa meekly nodded. "Bring it when you come back. Once you've cleaned up and put on some dry clothes, I'm tying you up in case you get any idea about escaping while I catch a few hours of sleep."

Forget *meek*. Hadn't she been cooperating? She tilted her face up to his. "You don't have to restrain me. I promise I won't try to go anywhere but the kitchen and bathroom."

"Either I tie you up or you're sleeping in this bed with me tonight."

The bald statement shocked her, and maybe not entirely in the way it should have. So what if he was the most manly thing she'd ever had in her apartment? He was the enemy. Her captor. Compassion for his injuries and this rudimentary attraction didn't matter. "You said you'd let me go."

"When I'm done with you, I will. I figure I need six to

eight hours of solid sleep to get my energy back before I can get out of your life. I can't risk you calling the cops or giving me away to anyone before I'm ready to leave. Until then, I'm tying you up." As if testing the newfound strength in his left hand, he closed his fingers around her chin and tipped it up, forcing her to look at him. "Do we understand each other?"

Teresa pulled away from his gentle yet firm, callused touch, nodding. "I'll get the tape."

Chapter Five

Nash turned his face away from the ribbon of sunlight that squeezed between the wall and curtains and hit him in the eyes.

He rolled over onto his back, moaning at the stiffness that made every joint ache. He raised his forearm to shield his eyes from the blinding glare of sunlight off the snow outside. Yeah, there was a chill on the bare skin of his torso. And yeah, he was pretty beat up. He could tell from the throbbing in his shoulder that he was far from 100 percent.

But he must have slept through the night. As consciousness pushed away the dregs of sleep, he was able to remember the echoes of his nightmares—familiar faces, doors closing all around him, locking him out, keeping him from reaching Axel Torres and Jim Richter and Tommy Delvecchio. And blood. Way too much blood. At least, that was how he interpreted the wispy clouds of scarlet hanging around him like warm breath in the wintry air of his dreams.

Despite the disturbing images that clung to the fringes of his thoughts, he felt a little more rested, a little more like a normal person. As normal as the last surviving member of a team marked for death could feel, at any rate.

That sobering thought raised him to another level of consciousness. He blinked his eyes beneath his arm, slowly taking stock of his surroundings. Sore thigh. Shoulder that felt as if it had been through a meat grinder. Soft quilt beneath his back. Softer pillow beneath his head. The subtle scents of alcohol and soap and…garlic? teased his nose. His stomach grumbled in a visceral response to the enticing aroma. Right. Food hadn't exactly been a priority for him these past two days. And whatever was cooking smelled mighty good.

Whatever was cooking?

No longer dreaming, no longer speculating, but wide-awake and suddenly aware of the keen gaze watching him, Nash opened his eyes and curled his fingers around the gun at his side before lowering his arm. He turned his head slightly to the right and saw that it was too late to go on the offensive.

"Ah, hell."

Teresa Rodriguez, that sweet little bundle of curves and sass, sat in the kitchen chair beside the bed, where he'd left her bound and gagged last night.

Except the tape he'd stuck loosely over her mouth was gone.

Not only was she free of her bindings, but she'd changed her clothes and held his badge and a magazine of bullets in either fist. "Good morning, Agent Nash."

Nash swung his legs off the side of the bed and sat up. Maybe a little too fast because her dark eyes and blue sweater swirled around in his vision. He shook off the dizziness, tossed aside the blanket she'd covered him with and spared the time to check his Smith & Wesson to confirm that the magazine she held came from his weapon. He was empty. At a distinct disadvantage. The captor was now the captive.

She bombarded him with questions before he could decide on his next plan of action. "Why did you make me afraid of you? Why did you kidnap me? Why didn't you just tell me the truth?"

That clever little minx. She'd cut herself loose from the duct tape he'd bound her wrists and ankles with last night. And while he couldn't stop the grin of admiration from hooking the corner of his mouth, he wasn't about to get her more involved with the mess that was his life right now than she already was. "It's complicated."

"Oh, I understand complicated. Why didn't you tell me you were a cop?" She leaned with him to keep them face-to-face when he tucked his empty weapon into the back of his jeans. "I would have helped you. I wouldn't have put up such a fuss. I thought you were a fugitive from the law—a drug dealer or a hit man. I was thinking of ways I could disable you long enough for me to get away. I almost sewed up a dirty wad of gauze in your wound to create a sepsis. If the pain and discomfort didn't slow you down, the resulting blood infection would eventually kill you."

She had plans to sabotage his injury? "Did you do that?"

"No. I took an oath to help people, not hurt them." So she had the brains to think like a survivalist, but she lacked the killer instinct to ensure her freedom by whatever means were available to her. That still gave him a slight edge over her because she had a heart and a conscience that restricted her actions, while he was willing to do whatever was necessary to complete his mission. "You should have told me the truth instead of bullying me. I grew up with cops. I understand the dangers they face. My brother's a cop. My sister Emilia is married to one."

He'd snatch that magazine of bullets right now if he

didn't think the room would start spinning again at the sudden movement. Nash didn't like feeling weak like this. He didn't like having his secrets exposed. And as much as he appreciated her resourcefulness, he didn't like that his hostage had turned the tables on him. He blinked her chocolate-brown eyes into clearer focus and let his gaze sweep down the clingy lines of her sweater and jeans. Nice. He'd been aware of those breasts and hips from the moment he'd pinned her body beneath his in the snow. But the rosy pink lips, adorned with nothing but accusation and shine, made him hungry for something more than food.

Priorities, Nash. He corrected the errant thought that warmed his blood. A man in survival mode didn't have time for fantasies like wondering what a woman would taste like beneath his kiss. At least she hadn't taken his gun or stolen another one from his go bag to aim at him. And he'd just have to take her word that she hadn't booby-trapped his wound to hasten his death. "What are you, a pickpocket?"

"I've developed certain skills over the years," she explained. "I'm the youngest of five children. I never could outmuscle AJ or outsmart Emilia and my sisters. So I developed a knack for being sneaky. I'd pocket a piece of a jigsaw puzzle or steal a couple of Mama's cookies so I could make sure I had my share of whatever they were doing before they were done."

Nash tapped his left front pocket, still trying to get his brain up to speed on the shifting situation. The cell phone was still there, nestled right next to the promised land. Could he have slept through her taking it off him? Had she already called 911 or turned him in to the brother or brother-in-law at KCPD she kept throwing at him? "How long have you been loose?"

"I waited a couple of hours until I was sure you were in a deep sleep. Then I crawled to the bathroom, got the scissors out of my sewing kit and cut myself free." She lifted her hand to the tiny pink welts and bruising that dotted her cheek. "I didn't realize how bad it would hurt to pull tape off my skin. The rest were easier."

"I tried to tape it to your clothes, not your skin." Feeling a pang of remorse for her getting hurt interfering with his annoyance, Nash instinctively reached out to touch his fingertips to the spot. A muscle quivered beneath the brush of his fingers, and her cool skin warmed. "I'm sorry."

"I wasn't exactly cooperating when you were restraining me."

"It's my fault, Peewee. Don't apologize or make excuses." What was it about good people getting hurt when he was around? Snatching his hand away, Nash pushed to his feet. And wobbled. Teresa immediately stood up to help him. He savored a moment of her steadying strength tucked to his side, then took advantage of her switching the badge and bullets to one hand by grabbing the magazine from her loose grip.

"Hey!"

He stepped away and pulled the gun from his belt, reloading it. Reclaiming a little more advantage. "I need my bag."

But turning around to survey the room forced him to grab the nearest bedpost as everything swayed.

"What am I going to do with you? Sometimes you really piss me off. Sometimes I feel sorry for you, and sometimes I even kind of like you. I don't understand you."

She'd get over it. "Where's my bag?"

Despite a sotto voce curse, her hand was at his elbow

again. "The dizziness is probably from blood loss and the fact that you haven't eaten anything for at least fourteen hours. I heated up some soup. It's my mama's chicken soup recipe—the best thing you can put in your stomach when you're not feeling a hundred percent."

"You made soup?" Now the smell of herbs and garlic made sense. His mouth watered at the deliciously homey aroma drifting through the apartment. Embarrassed by the answering grumble in his stomach when he was trying to be the tough guy and throw a little intimidation around, he searched the room for a clock. "How long have I been out?"

"About twelve hours." He pushed away her helping hand and staggered toward his bag near her dresser. "If you sit back down or come to the kitchen, I'll fix you a bowl."

"I need to get dressed."

She hurried past him and planted herself between him and the go bag. "You're running a low-grade fever. It may be your body's reaction to the hypothermia and trauma you went through yesterday. But it could also mean there's an infection setting in."

"I thought you said you didn't tamper with my wound."

"I didn't." She tipped her face up to his, her eyes flashing with temper. "You're managing that side effect all by yourself."

"I'm not going to any hospital." He watched her open those bow-shaped lips to argue. The desire to bend his head and silence that sassy mouth with his hit him like a punch to the gut. He must have a fever to forget for one moment the urgency of his mission. Instead of listening to his body, Nash snatched his badge from her hand and ignored both her arguments and that sirenlike pull she had on him. He tucked the wallet with his badge into the pocket beside his phone and reached down to pick up the bag.

But the moment he gritted his teeth and struggled to sling its heavy weight onto his shoulder, Teresa was there to help. She plucked the straps from his hand and carried it to the bed, where she set it on the rumpled blanket and unzipped it.

Nash had to slowly switch course to follow her. "Did you call anyone?"

She scooted away when he stepped up beside her to pull out a white T-shirt. Her arms were crossed in front of her and she was keeping her distance as he retrieved a snap-front Western shirt and gingerly started to dress in the clean clothes.

"You need a winter coat if you're going out," she groused, turning her head when he dropped his pants to pull on a fresh pair of briefs.

"I'm not staying here."

Nash pulled out his socks and sat on the edge of the bed. "Did you call anyone?" he repeated. He needed to know exactly how much lead time, if any, he had before this place would be swarming with KCPD officers or something worse.

"You conveniently destroyed all my phones, remember?" Her gaze lifted from the cord sticking out of the pocket of the jeans he wore, where he'd stashed the burner phone. "And I didn't want to get that close to you."

"You didn't call 911 on me? Didn't call big brother?" Bending over made him dizzy. Pulling his knee up to his chest to tug on one stupid sock nearly wore him out. Talk about being a sitting duck.

"No, Charlie. Charles? Agent Nash? What should I call you? Let me." With a noisy sigh, she dropped to her

knees in front of him to help him push up his pant legs
and put on his socks.

Hell. In addition to escaping and cooking and going
through his things, she'd washed and dried her long
hair. The long ponytail that fell down the middle of her
back was dark and shiny like a bay horse's well-brushed
coat. Double hell. He should be worried about the fact
he hadn't heard the water running in the next room or
awakened when she'd pulled those jeans and that fig-
ure-hugging sweater from a drawer or closet in here—
not wondering if her hair was as soft to the touch as her
skin had been.

And he damn sure shouldn't be wondering if she'd
bumped those compact yet decadent curves against him
when she'd been robbing him of his ammunition. Even
though she'd drawn the line at rummaging through his
pockets, she had to have practically lain on top of him to
reach over him to get the gun his fingers had been touching all night. At least, he thought he'd kept his weapon
beside him. But he was quickly learning there was little
he could predict about this woman.

Again he wondered why he couldn't have stuck himself with a meeker, more amenable captive to stitch him
up and hide him for a few hours. Stupid luck. Nurse
Teresa wasn't like any woman he'd been involved with
before. A man in his position should have minded his
misfortune a little more than he did.

"Nash. Everybody calls me Nash." He pointed to the
end of the bed, reminding them both who had the upper
hand—and the loaded gun—now. "Boots."

"You're in no shape to walk out of here. And you don't
have a car." She picked up his Justin boots and helped
him pull them onto his feet. But she stopped in the middle of tugging his jeans over the shaft of his left boot.

"Unless you plan to steal mine?" She tilted her face to his, her cheeks flooding with heat. "You're stealing my car?" Then she was standing up, backing away. "I *am* reporting you. I was dumb to think you needed a second chance. I unloaded the electronics from my armoire, so I can go anytime I want to. I think I can outrun you in the shape you're in."

"Wait." She spun toward the door, but Nash grabbed her by the arm and pulled her back. She landed on his lap.

"Let go of me." He grunted when she put her hand against his bandaged thigh and tried to push away. "Sorry."

But his pain didn't stop her from scrambling to get away. She just changed tactics, swatting a fist at his good shoulder but avoiding doing the damage she should have by going after his injuries and freeing herself. Still, she was enough of a handful that Nash caught her flailing arms at her sides and pulled her against his chest. Anchoring her in place sapped his strength, but he refused to let her go. If she got away from him and made it to Mrs. Walker's apartment or some other neighbor's phone and brought the local cops down on him…

"Please, darlin', I need you to stop."

Please? Now who was lacking the killer instinct? Now her boots were aiming for his shins and the side of her hip kept brushing against his groin. *You don't have time for this. Tie her up again. Make her cooperate. You owe it to Tommy and Richter and Torres.* "How much is your car worth?"

"What?" Curiosity made the twisting stop. She settled on top of his thighs and looked up at him as if this was some kind of embrace instead of a snare. "I don't know. My brother's the car nut. I bought it for a few thousand dollars when I graduated from nursing school and he put a new engine in it for me. I don't know what he paid. It was a gift."

Risking another bolt to the door, Nash released his grip on her waist to reach inside his bag and pull out his flash wad of rolled-up bills. Her eyes widened as he counted out ten hundreds and pushed the cash into her hand. "Is this enough to borrow it for twenty-four hours?"

Teresa jumped to her feet, tossing the money back at him as if it burned her fingers. "Oh, my God. You're a dirty cop? How much money do you have in there?"

The sanctimonious accusation stung more than it should have. He retrieved the scattered bills and set them in a neat pile on her bed. "You ought to know. My badge was in the same pocket."

"I was looking for another phone. I didn't even touch the other pistol or shotgun or boxes of ammunition in there. Once I found your badge and that little black book…"

His contact book?

Any truce between them had just ended. He dove back into the bag. It wasn't there. "Teresa?"

She realized her mistake a moment too late and darted toward the bedroom door. Nash was on his feet in an instant, lurching forward as the room tilted. Damn it. She *could* outrun him.

But even in his condition, she couldn't outmuscle him. He looped his arm around the waist, lifting her off the floor. Yet he was too off balance still to simply hold her against him, so he let his momentum back her into the wall and trapped her there with his body. She braced her hands against his chest, defiantly tipping her chin. "Stop grabbing me, you big bully."

But the contact book was nonnegotiable. "Uh-uh, darlin'. You're not going anywhere. Where is it?"

"Stop doing that."

He felt her up, patted her down, checked every pocket until he found the book tucked in the rear of her jeans and he pulled it out. He waved the leather book in her face. "Who did you call?"

"No one. You trashed all my phones and the cords were in your pants.

He wasn't buying it. If she'd looked through the pages of names and notes and numbers, then she already knew too much. Cartel names. Notes about his team's murders. A list of potential suspects masquerading as coworkers. Any one of whom might want him dead. The idea that she might already know too much made him sick to his stomach. "Some of the people who want me dead are in here. Who did you call?"

The tone of his voice changed from a threat to a very real concern. Her fingers curled into the front of his shirt, pleading with him, and the struggles stopped. He hoped. Something was stirring behind his zipper, and it wasn't the instinct to defend himself. He still held her suspended above the floor, his hips wedged into the cradle of hers. As he regained control of his fears, he realized his fingers had tunneled into the velvety length of her ponytail. Yes, it was as soft and thick as he'd imagined, it smelled cleaner than any horse he knew, and he was a fool to let this crazy heat she ignited in him distract him for even one moment.

"Teresa." He let her toes slide to the floor but didn't release her. "Whose name did you pull out of this book?"

Her fingertips pulsed against his chest. Was she afraid of him? Perhaps soothing the wounded beast? Was this the nurse trying to take care of him again? Or was she as vividly aware of each ragged exhale pushing their bodies against each other as he was? Was she just as baffled by the electricity arcing between them?

"Technically, I didn't call anyone."

"But...?"

She tilted her dark eyes up to his. "My internet comes through the cable line. I sent an email to the name with the star at the front of your book. Jesse Puente. I searched for his name online and it said he worked at the DEA like you do. So I emailed him."

Nash dropped his forehead to hers and swore a blue streak. Then he pulled away from the grasp of her hands, arming himself, getting ready to leave. She clung to the wall beside the bedroom door but watched his every move. "He said you were a good cop. I'm an idiot for trusting him, aren't I? I wanted to justify you kidnapping me, so I believed him. I took him at his word because I needed to make sense of everything my gut is telling me about you."

Nash fastened his belt and holstered his gun. "What nonsense is your gut telling you?"

"That you're not really a bad guy. Even if you're a bad cop, there has to be a good reason why you've made whatever choices you've made and why you have all that cash." She pushed away from the wall and blocked his path again. "If you were really a criminal without a conscience, you'd have shot at me instead of that tree behind your truck last night. You wouldn't have cared if the duct tape pulled my skin or stuck to my clothes. I think there's good in you. Or believe me, I'd have been long gone before you woke up this morning."

Chapter Six

I think there's good in you.

Well, if that didn't sound a lot like the counselors at the Texas boys ranch where Nash had grown up. He'd been so angry after his parents' murders, resentful that he'd been stuck in some remote patch of sandy grassland filled with hard work and horse manure. He'd started and finished his share of fights and wrestled with his own vengeful tendencies enough that it was easy to draw on the experience of his youth whenever he needed to assume a less-than-savory undercover identity. The men and women who worked the land, ran the school and counseled the troubled boys and teens there had worked a miracle on him, inspiring him to get his act together to get through school and become a cop.

But every now and then—when his closest friends were being murdered, when innocent lives were being destroyed and he couldn't do a damn thing about it, when the woman he loved said she couldn't handle his life and walked away—those masochistic demons would reappear.

He'd need some time to process Teresa's opinion of him. Seeing him as anything positive, as someone she might trust, was just wishful thinking on her part. He was on a mission to find out the truth about the traitor who'd gotten his team killed—or he was going to die trying. It was whatever he needed, when he needed it. His life was all about survival and hard choices right now—not sexual attraction or guilty consciences or idealistic guts that had the wrong impression about him. Nash was afraid there'd be more casualties like Tommy Delvecchio before he got to the truth. But as long as he got the job done, he didn't care.

There wasn't anything good about that.

He clipped his badge back on his belt where it belonged. "What did Puente say?"

Teresa recoiled half a step, hugging her arms around her waist when he dismissed her overture of trust and support. "He thanked me for contacting him. I thought I was helping. Did I get you into trouble?"

A little bit, darlin'. "Where's your computer?"

"In the living room."

"I need to see it."

It hurt to do it, but Nash lifted the bag onto his uninjured shoulder and stalked down the hallway after her. The main rooms smelled like Christmas with the fragrant pine needles on her tree and the scents of home cooking filling the apartment. Taking stock of his surroundings in daylight, Nash shook his head. Teresa had not only emptied out the armoire, but she'd shoved it back into place, away from the door. He'd been a sitting duck for several hours, plenty of time for the mole in his department to find that email to Captain Puente and track it back to its source.

While she sat at the computer desk behind her couch to turn on the machine, Nash pushed aside the hodgepodge of toys and other gifts, wrapping paper and ribbons on the dining room table and set his bag down. He checked the front window and peephole of the door. Everything was still locked down, and nobody appeared to be showing more interest in her fourth-floor apartment than they should be. Reassured there wasn't a pending home invasion, at least, he crossed to stand behind her chair.

"Show me the messages," he ordered.

Teresa pulled up her email account. Nash leaned over her shoulder to read her message to the captain.

Dear Mr. Puente—I have a man here with ID that says his name is Charles Nash. He's badly wounded, but I've taken care of his injuries. I don't have a picture to send, but he's about 6'3", muscular, has dark blond/light brown hair and needs a shave. He has scarring on his left arm and back. To be honest, they look like knife cuts and a bullet wound. Is he really a DEA agent? Is he working a case for you here in Kansas City? He's warned me several times not to contact the police, but I found your name in his bag and took a chance that you could help me.

He hasn't hurt me yet, but there have been plenty of threats. Please advise before I turn him over to the authorities here. He asked me not to, which makes me wonder if he's telling me the truth.

He doesn't know I'm writing you. I don't know how long I have before he wakes up, so I'd appreciate a quick reply. Sorry to contact you this way, but I don't have access to a phone.

Thank you.
Teresa Rodriguez, R.N.

After he nodded to her, she clicked on Captain Puente's alleged reply.

Dear Ms. Rodriguez,
Sounds like the Charlie Nash I know. You say he's in-

jured—have you taken him to a hospital for proper care? I'd like to follow up on his condition because yes, he's working an important case for me, and if he's out of commission, I need to replace him on the investigation.

Rest assured, you are safe with him. He's a good man, if a bit of a loose cannon sometimes.

As soon as you can reach a phone, please call me at this number to verify your identity and confirm Nash's badge number. Thank you.

Captain Jesse Puente
Houston Office
DEA

Nash read the phone number at the bottom of the email. Puente's direct line. Was that significant? Why not simply request a reply to his email? Why not instruct Teresa to call the general office to get whoever was on duty, or notify the local cops to request backup for an injured officer?

While sorting out possibilities, Nash rubbed his jaw, massaging the stubble there. He needed a shave. He needed some food. He checked the clock on the computer and the time stamp of the two emails. Almost three hours old. Plenty of time to catch a flight to K.C. He needed to get out of here. But things had just gotten more complicated. He needed to come up with a plan F or G now.

"Have you made any other contact with the captain?" Nash asked.

Teresa shook her head. "I heard you moving in the bedroom. You must have been having a nightmare. But I didn't want to risk you waking up and catching me out here. So I shut the computer down and went back to watch you sleep."

The nightmare was the same whether he was asleep or awake. Nash pushed away from the chair. "There's no proof that it was Puente who got the message. Anyone could have answered that."

She followed him across the living room, rubbing her arms as though she was cold. "He made me think I could trust you. Should I have emailed my brother instead?"

"If it was me, I would have run out that door." He nodded toward the television and sound equipment on the floor. "Your survival instincts are on the fritz. You had the means to escape. To turn me in. Why didn't you?"

"If you didn't have me, you might take Mrs. Walker or someone else in the building hostage. I can deal with you better than an old woman or a young family can."

"Deal?"

"Yes." She moved into the kitchen to stir the soup. "If Mrs. Walker knew about the guns in your bag and all the blood you were hiding under that blanket, she'd probably have a heart attack. If you're a good guy and need help, I have connections no one else in this building has. If it turns out you're a bad cop, I can put up a better fight than anyone else. So you're stuck with me."

Nash stopped at the kitchen peninsula, breathing in the fragrant meal simmering on the stove. "You're a lot of trouble, you know that, Teresa Rodriguez?"

"I know." Her agreeable response surprised him. She covered the pot and held up her hands, showing she had no hot liquid or dangerous utensils on her as she circled the counter to join him. "That's my nickname. *Gamberro.*" The Spanish word for *troublemaker.* "I've been called that my entire life."

So his wasn't the only life she'd turned sideways? He settled onto the nearest stool, bringing his height closer to hers. "Who calls you that?"

"My older brother and sisters. My mother, when she was alive. I'm too impulsive. I have a temper. I lead with my heart."

"You get yourself into trouble before you figure out a way to get out of it." *Like stopping to help a stranded motorist on a wintry night.*

Nash felt a little of that same chill that had her rubbing her arms for warmth again. "They make me feel like a child. But I'm twenty-nine years old. I have skills and talents I need to use. I can do more with my life than be taken care of. I've dealt with some horrible things as I've grown up. I don't need to be protected from everything."

"Yeah, you do." Although he wondered how her idea of "horrible things" stacked up against his murdered parents and violent youth, he didn't have time for curiosity or compassion. "The moment Captain Puente or whoever's impersonating him opened that email in Houston, a clock started ticking."

"What does that mean?"

He might as well spell it out since, as far as he was concerned, they were in this together now. "I'm an undercover agent, Peewee. I supervise a team of agents who've infiltrated a drug war. Only my cover's been blown. So were theirs. By a crooked cop or someone else on the take in the Houston office."

Her eyes widened in shock. "The men who tried to kill you were cops?"

"I doubt the three goons who came after me yesterday were actual cops, but they're definitely working with one. No one except for the people in my office knew I was heading for Kansas City. Yet the cartel thugs who shot me up and murdered a friend didn't just track me to my location. They were waiting for me."

Her soft gasp barely registered. "You lost a friend yesterday?"

"A rookie agent. He was trying to help me." Nash's wry laugh elicited a frown. "Maybe I should have you contact your brother—see if KCPD has had a report of four dead bodies at a chop-shop near the river. They could at least get Tommy back to his family in Houston." Any urge to laugh, even with that raw sarcasm, was crushed beneath the load of guilt he carried. "I didn't even hold his hand or check to see if he was killed instantly. I just... There were too many bullets flying. I had to leave him behind."

And now her hand was on his arm—comforting him? Seeing an opportunity to finagle her own rescue? "I can do that. If you give me back the cords to connect my phones, I'll gladly call AJ and find out if he knows anything about your friend."

Nash shook his head. "Just kidding, Peewee. No cops."

She pulled her hand away. "I don't understand. Clearly you're upset. AJ can help. If I ask—"

"No." Even if her brother had good intentions, it'd be too big a risk to take. "Someone at Houston HQ is funneling sensitive information to the Graciela cartel. I'm the only survivor of three different hits. Until I can identify the mole in our office, I'm off the grid. At least, I was until someone in Houston read your email. There are warring factions within the cartel, and both sides want me dead—I get that. But knowing someone I trusted leaked our names and locations? I intend to live long enough to find out who betrayed my men."

"And you. He betrayed you, too." Man, she was still feeling sorry for him.

He'd get her over that real quick. "Now your name is

on that hit list, too. Every bad thing you think about me? Those cartel thugs are worse."

"What did I do?"

He pointed to the computer. "You sent an email that can lead the traitor straight to Kansas City. Straight to this apartment. Straight—"

"To me." She sank onto the stool beside him, her skin turning pale beneath its warm olive tone. "You think they'll come after me to find you?"

"Yep."

"Can't you just call this Captain Puente to see if he's the one who got the email?"

"What if he's the traitor?" Nash had been proud to get assigned to Captain Puente's team, had always considered the older officer a straight shooter. But then, he'd thought the best of every man on their undercover unit... until his friends had died, and the only explanation that made sense was a mole on the inside who'd leaked their names to the cartels.

Teresa's knuckles turned white where she gripped the counter. "There isn't anyone you can trust?"

"I'm flying solo on this. At least, I was until you picked me up." Knowing he was wasting precious time and energy caring about her distress, he slid his hand across the counter to rest it over both of hers anyway. There was only so much guilt a man could bear. "That's why I didn't want you to call the local cops or your big brother. That's why I didn't want to go to the hospital. They're all red flags to where I'm hiding out that I'm not ready to put up yet."

Her grip on the counter relaxed, but she didn't pull away. "You need to get better before you deal with those horrible men."

"I don't have that luxury. But I do need to stay ahead

of these guys. I need to get some leads and pinpoint who set us up before they strike again. If I die, they'll get away with murdering my men. I'm the only one who knows the leak came from our office. That's why they're looking for me. Once I'm gone, the bastard who gave up my team can go right on selling information to the cartels." She shook her head and started to pull away, but Nash curled his fingers around hers, apologizing, reassuring, warning her of the danger. "And since they're going to be looking for you now, too…"

"You're not going to let me go, are you?"

"Nope. Rule Two, remember? Protect your assets." He threaded the fingers of his left hand through the velvety strands of coffee-colored hair that had fallen over her shoulder. "I thought I could use you to patch me up enough to keep me going a few days longer. If I kept you from asking questions, if I kept things anonymous, you'd stay an innocent bystander and I could leave without making you a target. None of the people after me would even know of your existence. But that's all changed now. You're part of my team now. I'm not going to lose anybody else to these bastards. Especially a sweet thing like you." Her chin tipped up with a jerk at the offhand compliment. Barely noticing the twinge in his shoulder, he pulled his fingers down through the length of her hair before letting her go and nodding to the kitchen. "You got a thermos or something you can pack up some soup in? Get an overnight bag with whatever you need for a few days."

She gathered her ponytail and flipped it behind her back as she pushed to her feet. "I have a job. I have plans for Christmas. I can't go with you."

"Right now mine's the only plan you have to worry about. You're going to need my protection."

"That sounds like a really desperate pickup line."

"The only thing desperate is the situation. I can't let you go until I find this guy, but I won't let you get hurt. I give you my word."

"Your word?" She went into the kitchen and turned off the burner beneath the soup. "Forgive me if I don't jump at the chance to go on the lam with you."

"There isn't anybody who can vouch for me right now. But when I make a promise, I keep it. I know it's a huge leap of faith, considering how I've treated you. But I will keep you safe. What does your heart tell you about me?"

Her eyes locked on to his for an endless moment. Yeah, he'd been listening when she said she led with her heart instead of listening to common sense. And yes, he would play on that weakness of hers to ensure her cooperation. "This...mole would really come after me?"

"You're his best lead to finding me."

Teresa nodded slowly, as if evaluating her options. "And you'd probably die of infection or pop those stitches and bleed out without me to take care of you."

Possibly.

"Would I be your partner or your captive?"

"Depends on how well you cooperate, *Gamberro*."

"Don't call me that. Peewee is bad enough." And then the energy in the room shifted. She squatted down and disappeared while he heard her rummaging through a cabinet. "I actually only have one day I'm scheduled between now and Christmas because I'm working the holiday. But Christmas Day is nonnegotiable. I'm planning a party for the patients who'll be hospitalized over the holiday. I have presents and cookies and decorations. I could only help you through Christmas Eve."

"Teresa, this isn't a negotiation. I can't leave you—"

"I won't disappoint those children. I suppose I could

call someone to take my shift tomorrow and clear the trade with my supervisor." The cabinet door closed and a thermos appeared before she popped up to face him over the counter. "If I had a phone."

Nash tapped his cell in his pocket, wondering how many other saps had succumbed to that sweetly innocent smile of hers, which he suspected wasn't so innocent at all. Yet he was actually toying with giving the phone to her. "I suppose I could trust you enough for one call. But only with me listening in."

"Partner or captive?" she pressed.

A knock on her apartment door startled them both. "Teresa, are you in there?"

She set down the thermos at the man's deep, slightly accented voice. "AJ?"

Nash pulled his weapon and stood. "Big brother the cop, AJ?"

She'd tricked him again.

Chapter Seven

Nash grabbed Teresa by the arm to keep her from hurrying past him to the door. His voice was a furious whisper. "I thought you said you didn't contact anybody else."

"I didn't."

Screw that innocent act. Why had he not seen this coming? "You set me up. All this chitchat was a stall until he could get here."

"No. I swear." She splayed her hand against his chest, her eyes wide, her voice hushed. "Put your gun away. Please. I don't know why AJ's here, but he can help us. We'll just tell him the truth. He can give you protection. Put you in a safe house."

Nash's voice was equally toneless and urgent. "If I had a little sister that some desperate man had kidnapped, I don't think I'd be willing to listen to any explanations before I slapped the cuffs on him and threw his butt in a jail cell." He leaned down to whisper against her ear. "Where I'd be easy pickings for Graciela's and Vargas's hit squads, by the way."

"Hit squads?"

He raised his head enough for her to see he was dead serious. "If they think you know anything about me—about my investigation or where I'm hiding—they won't be nice about how they get the information out of you.

And if I'm in a holding cell or even an interview room, I won't be able to protect you."

The color blanched from her cheeks before she turned her head to another knock on the door. "I swear I didn't contact him."

"Tía Teresa, I have some visitors for you." AJ Rodriguez sounded patient, cajoling, not at all like a big brother bent on smashing the man who'd endangered his sister.

"Tía Teresa," a child's voice called. "Did Santa come to your house?" Someone even younger laughed.

"My nephews." Teresa's fingertips pinched the skin beneath Nash's shirt as she held on tighter. "Please, put the gun away. AJ will be armed, too, and I don't want my family to get hurt. I'll get rid of them."

Nash's thumb rubbed tiny circles in the wool of her sleeve as he evaluated her sincerity.

Another knock, and the tenor of AJ's voice had changed. "Teresa, are you in there? Is everything all right?"

"I'm fine," she shouted, the volume of her voice jarring to Nash's ears. "I just need a minute." She dropped her voice to a whisper again. "If you expect me to trust everything you've told me, then you'll have to trust me first."

Big brother knocking at the door wasn't leaving Nash much choice. "Teresa?" AJ called.

"One wrong word," Nash warned, "and this could get ugly fast."

"I won't give you away. I promise."

With a curt nod and a refusal to holster his weapon, Nash pried her hand from his shirt and ducked behind the armoire, where he could peek through the back to watch the door open without being seen. Smoothing her sweater back into place and taking a deep breath, Teresa opened the door. "What? Is the building on fire? I said I was coming. *Buenos días,* AJ."

She beamed a smile and traded a hug and a kiss with the stocky dark-haired man. That compact size must run in the family. AJ might be only five-nine or so, but he was built like a fighter. His badge flashed from a chain around his neck in the opening of his padded leather jacket. And despite the small hand clutched in his, the detective was carrying at least one sidearm. Nash lowered his gun to his side, pointing it away from their visitors but keeping himself ready to move if he needed to.

"Claire." Teresa exchanged a hug with a beautiful blonde who carried a mini Michelin Man on her hip. "And my two favorite boys. Tony and little Adam." There were noisy kisses for the toddler stuffed into a snowsuit and the older boy, who held on to his father's hand. "What brings you here this morning?"

Nash didn't get another look before Teresa scooted them all out into the hall and pulled the door behind her, leaving it ajar just enough that he could hear the entire conversation.

"You're not inviting us in?" AJ asked.

The woman called Claire, AJ's wife, Nash assumed, answered in an oddly toned yet articulate voice. "I told you we should have called first. Maybe she has a guest."

"No guests," Teresa assured them. Then she lowered her voice to a fake whisper. "But plenty of secrets. Santa stopped by for an early visit this week and asked me to wrap up some goodies for him and hold them until he's back to pick them up on Christmas Eve. I can't let you into Santa's workshop, now, can I?"

"I told you Tía Teresa was helping Santa." The little boy named Tony sounded quite certain of his holiday rules. "We can't peek, Daddy, or Santa will know, and he won't bring the presents to our house. We have to go."

Although he could imagine the little boy tugging on his father's hand, the prolonged silence made Nash wonder if AJ was doubting Teresa's whimsical story of aiding and abetting the bearded little elf in the red suit. Nash wished he had eyes on the scene, to make sure there were no coded messages being exchanged.

"You're wrapping presents?" AJ finally asked. The doubtful inflection in his tone made Nash think no SOS signals had gone up.

"I am. I've even got one for you, big brother. And you're hard to surprise, so no coming in." Nash saw Teresa's hand reach for the doorknob behind her to keep the view into her apartment blocked. "Not that I don't love seeing all of you, but why are you here?"

"We were just a few blocks away," her brother explained. "Tony had a basketball game this morning. We thought you'd like to join us for lunch."

"Normally, I would, but…" she slurred her voice through clenched teeth "…there is a lot of work to do." Then she was speaking normally again. "Did you win your game?"

"No." Tony's pout was audible. "But I did make a basket."

"That's great," Teresa cheered. "And you'll get them next—"

Claire interrupted. "Tony's game was all the way out in Oak Grove." Nash was beginning to think the woman might be hearing impaired, from the unique quality of her voice. But that didn't stop her from being an active part of the conversation. "What your brother really wanted was to see with his own eyes that you're all right."

"All right?" Teresa feigned innocence very well. "Why wouldn't I be all right?"

"KCPD got a report on a truck shot up on Lee's Summit Road last night." AJ Rodriguez was definitely a cop. Nash recognized the direct, no-nonsense demeanor. "I know you take that route home from work, even though I've told you to use a safer, well-lit route when it's late. Especially in this weather. You know the city doesn't clear that road as often as the main routes."

"I did take that road home after I did some shopping last night," Teresa confessed. She was smart, mixing in enough of the truth to make her lies sound plausible. "There were a couple of slick spots, but the snow wasn't an issue for me."

"Did you see anything?" AJ asked. "Dispatch got a call from a woman about the truck. She never identified herself. They got disconnected before the dispatcher could get an ID."

Nash held his breath, waiting to hear her answer.

"So of course you assume it was me." Nash recognized the defensive bristle in Teresa's voice. "Like no other drivers would be on that road?"

Nash hadn't seen much traffic except for her sedan. He'd been lucky she'd stopped.

"I tried calling you this morning and there was no answer."

"I lost my cell."

AJ wasn't giving up on this. "I called the landline, too."

"I had a late night. I unplugged the phones so I could sleep in. I knew one of my siblings would be checking up on me this morning."

AJ remained coolly unruffled, despite the growing tension in his baby sister's tone. "You didn't see anything? I got a look at that truck this morning. There was nothing in it except for blood on the seat. There were tracks from more than one vehicle at the side of the road, and multiple footprints in the snow."

Nash could count the seconds of silence as Teresa hesitated. This was it. He wondered how good she was at lying to her family—or if this was the moment when she tossed him over to the enemy. "Well, I did see a black truck in the ditch and thought I could help, but...it was already empty when I got there. The driver must have hitched a ride."

"You went up to a stranger's truck? Alone?" Nash heard a low-pitched curse in Spanish. "Teresa, there's a BOLO out for the owner of that truck."

Be on the lookout for the driver in question. *Him.* Nash clenched his teeth to stifle his own curse. The mole in Houston must have listed him nationwide as some kind of fugitive.

"Why?" Teresa asked.

"Usually, when there's that much blood, we look for a body to go with it."

"Antonio." Claire chided her husband, probably not wanting their children to hear details like that.

"I saw an accident on the side of the road, AJ," Teresa insisted. "I'm a nurse. I'm expected to help if someone's injured."

"At the hospital." So Teresa's independent streak could get under her big brother's skin, as well. "No one expects you to risk your life on a dangerous road in the middle of the night."

"*I* expect it of me." Her temper was brewing. "I'm okay. I didn't see..." Nash tensed. *Don't hesitate, darlin'. He'll know you're lying.* "There was no one in the truck. I'm all in one piece. See for yourself. Claire, a little help here? I'm sorry I have to turn down the lunch invitation, but I have things I need to take care of today."

"There was a *lot* of blood, Teresa. The truck had out-of-state plates and, did I mention, bullet holes?" Nash held his breath while AJ pushed Teresa for the truth. "You take foolish—"

"Antonio. *Amo,*" Claire interrupted in a quiet voice. "Your sister is fine. She's also grown-up. She has a job to do, just like you and me. We need to go and give her her space. Come on, boys, tell your aunt goodbye."

"Bye-bye," the little one chirped.

"Bye, Tía Teresa," Tony echoed.

There was a rustle of hugs and goodbyes.

And one last warning from her brother. "If you run into something like that again, you call me before you take matters into your own hands. *¿Comprendes?*"

"Entiendo." Yes, she understood.

"I'm trying to take care of you," AJ insisted.

"And I was trying to take care of the injured driver."

"I know, little one. But you could have run into a dangerous man. You give me cause to worry, yes?" There was a momentary pause, then, "I love you."

Judging by her muffled voice, there was another hug. "I love you, too."

And then the door was closing and Teresa threw the dead bolt.

Nash crept out of his hiding place to find her leaning against the door with her eyes shut. "You okay?" he asked.

Her eyes popped open to meet his gaze. "I got rid of them, like you said. Endured the lecture, lied to my family. It's all good," she added, her sarcasm evident in her tone.

"I get the idea your brother knows you're lying."

"Well, it's the first time I've harbored a fugitive, so I wasn't quite sure what to say."

"Teresa..." Maybe she was partner material after all. Nash holstered his gun, surprised at how well she'd covered for him. But it might not be enough. The tiny dots of bruising beside her mouth were a clear indication to even a bad detective that something wasn't quite right in Teresa's world. "There are other reasons why law enforcement might issue a BOLO besides looking for a criminal. Maybe someone in Houston filed a missing-person report on me."

Her gaze flashed up to his. "Do you think that's what happened?"

Honestly? Nash shook his head, wishing he had a better reassurance to give her. "Your brother sounded too worried about you."

"AJ always worries." Teresa tapped her thumb against her chest. "*Trouble,* remember?"

He hated that she joked about herself. Ignoring the urgency of the situation and the instincts that warned him her brother was a hard man to fool, Nash stroked his fingertips across the injury again. "I'm sorry. I wish I didn't need you to do this for me."

"I wish I could believe you." Her dark lashes fluttered against her cheeks at his touch. Man, he was taking liberties he had no right to. He didn't have time to care about anything except finishing this job and avenging the deaths of his men. But this woman who was full of surprises stunned him again when she turned her face into the cup of his hand, turning his comfort into a caress. "I've seen your injuries. If nothing else, I do believe you need me."

Nash let his fingertips slide into the edge of her hair.

"What you did for me last night was a brave thing. You knew you could help, and you did."

She smiled up at him, easing a little of his guilt before pulling away and leaving his palm tingling with the imprint of her cool skin pressed against his. She headed for the kitchen. "You didn't give me a choice."

"Take the compliment, darlin'. You didn't have to stop on that empty stretch of road. And I'm still alive, so you must be doing something right."

"Thank you for saying that." She pulled a ladle from a crock beside the stove and pointed it at him. "This is all going to turn out right in the end, isn't it?"

Nash was done lying to her. "I can't make that kind of guarantee."

She held his gaze for several seconds longer before her eyes shuttered and she went to work.

While she packed them some food, Nash sorted through his go bag, taking stock of his gear and prepping another magazine of bullets. "You're protecting AJ and his family, too. Remember that. I'm sure lying to your family sucks, but the fewer people who know about me, the better for both of us."

"I know. I'll pack some medical supplies, too. And you still need a winter coat."

"We'll buy one somewhere along the way. And a hat." A real Stetson to replace the one he'd sacrificed would take too much of his cash. But Kansas City had been a stockyard town back in the day—there had to be some knockoff cowboy hats for sale somewhere.

"There's a Chiefs stocking cap in the front closet you can borrow," she offered. "It's not too girly."

Nash went to the closet and pulled out her coat and the stocking cap he found in a basket on the top shelf. The red and gold clashed with his Texans football spirit, but sporting the local team's colors would certainly help him blend in in K.C. He pulled the knit cap over his head. "This'll do for now."

"Is that what your money's for? Coats and hats?"

"It's for whatever we need. I always keep a stash when I'm undercover so I don't have to use credit cards or ATMs that can be traced." He got out his phone and met her at the sink. If they were going to be a team, with her following his orders to the letter, then he was going to show her a little of that trust she'd asked for. He pulled her hand away from the dish towel she held and placed the cell in her palm, curling her fingers around it and holding on. "Call your supervisor and someone to cover your shift. Do everything I say, and I promise I will keep you alive. And I'll do my damnedest to solve this case and have you home to your family and that hospital party by Christmas."

She nodded, accepting the deal. He hoped. She pulled away, crossing to the dismantled wall phone to open the thick directory beneath it. "What about your family, Nash? Are they safe from the men who are after you? Do you need to warn them?"

"Ain't nobody at home to call, Peewee. It's one of the hazards of the job. No parents. No siblings. No girl-friend..." *Phone calls.* A nagging suspicion, one that should have registered sooner, finally worked its way through the pain and guilt and low-grade fever. He followed her to the phone book. "Why didn't your brother mention your cell phone? You said you lost it, but I trashed it and left it on the floor of my truck. If he saw the blood in the seat, he would have seen that, too."

Teresa shrugged. "AJ said there was nothing inside."

Nash processed all the possible explanations, not liking a one of them. "So who cleaned up after we left?"

"The police?"

"AJ's the police. If they found your cell, they could get your number from the computer chip inside. He'd know it was yours."

She nodded, understanding his concern. "And if he knew that was my phone, especially in pieces like that, he'd have been on my case even more. Especially if he found it in a truck belonging to someone the police are looking for."

"Someone else beat the cops to it." And that someone could already be en route to Teresa's apartment.

With a renewed urgency pumping through his blood, Nash crossed the living room to peek outside through the blinds again. He'd checked earlier for anything that seemed suspicious, but he was noting the details now. There was some slow-moving traffic, but the block was too long and there were too many trees along the winding road to know if anyone was circling around for a closer look. There were two parking lot entrances to Teresa's place. Seventeen cars parked there and at the curb in front. More in the lot for the apartments across the street.

"Is something wrong?" Teresa's voice at his shoulder startled him. "You're scaring me a little bit."

A bundled-up man was sweeping snow off the sidewalk across the street, showing no interest in anything except his task. Nash looked for occupied vehicles. A van in the parking lot had a mom strapping a child into a car seat in the back. The wind shifted, blowing the exhaust away from a black SUV parked across the street, revealing a dark-haired man behind the wheel, talking on his cell.

Nash didn't startle when Teresa touched his arm, although his pulse still kicked into a higher gear. "What is it?"

He pulled her off to the side of the window, keeping her out of sight as he pointed out the black vehicle. "Is that your brother?"

She peeked through the blinds. "No. I don't know who that is. AJ drives a Trans Am. Or Claire's red Escalade when they have the kids."

Taking her hand, Nash pulled her into step behind him. "Come on. We need to go." He tossed Teresa her coat and hoisted his bag onto his good shoulder. "Is there a back entrance we can use to get to the parking lot?"

"Sure." She slipped into her coat, pulled a backpack from the closet and loaded it with the thermos and food. Nash picked up her purse and dropped the whole thing into the knapsack's main compartment when she started to pull out certain items, hurrying her along. "Do you think that man is here to kill you?"

"I'm not waiting around to find out. Let's go."

She stopped tying the backpack and snapped her fingers. "The first-aid kit."

When she dashed past him, he grabbed her hand again and turned her toward the door. "We don't have time. Vargas's and Graciela's thugs travel in packs."

"Packs?" Her fingers shook as she unlocked the door.

"If that's a cartel man, I don't know where his partner is. He might already be in the building." Nash entered the hallway first, scanning both directions to make sure they were alone while she locked her door behind him. The elevator at the front of the building hummed to life as the gears in the shaft engaged. Not good. "Someone's on their way up."

Teresa nodded toward the opposite end of the hall. "The back stairs are down there."

When she started to walk, Nash pressed his hand to the small of her back and hurried her into a jog. "Move it, darlin'." The elevator might not be coming to the fourth floor, but no sense taking any chances on being seen. "Rule Three—avoiding a confrontation beats fighting your way out of one. I won't get caught in the middle of a shoot-out with you here."

"I'm okay with that rule."

They were cutting this too close. "No wonder your brother didn't ask you any questions about my truck."

"What do you mean?" She reached the stairwell door and shoved it open.

He scooted in right after her. "KCPD would have run the Texas plates and ID'd that truck as mine. An alert would have gone over the wire. Headquarters in Houston should have answered the alert by identifying me as an agent, one in need of assistance with that blood on the scene."

"AJ didn't ask me any questions about the accident. If he'd suspected a fellow cop was in danger, he'd have asked me for details about what I'd seen. He wouldn't have gone ballistic about me trying to help. He didn't know your truck belonged to a cop." The woman was smart. Thankfully, she was also sharp enough to check over the railing before heading down the stairs. "The mole in your office must have gotten that alert. And labeled you a fugitive."

"Or buried it without a response." Nash waited to peer through the closing crack of the door as the elevator opened. The dark-haired man he'd spotted out front stepped out. That bulge beneath his coat wasn't his cell phone. The guy was armed. Despite the bandaged graze in Nash's thigh, his legs felt solid as he raced down the stairs behind Teresa. "The cartels already have someone else here."

"That guy out front?"

"The guy knocking on your apartment door right now."

"My...?" When she stopped at the first-floor exit and spun around, he nearly plowed into her. "My email must have... What did I—?"

"Forget it." The fear or apology or whatever had widened those beautiful dark eyes was too much. He palmed the back of her neck, tipped her face up and pressed a quick kiss to her mouth. "None of this is your fault." When her lips softened beneath his, he lifted her onto her toes and leaned in to kiss her again. "None of it."

The second kiss was almost as quick. But firmer. More satisfying. Less like an apology and more like a man testing his welcome with a woman he cared about.

And she wasn't pushing him away.

He heard her soft catch of breath, felt her palm bracing against the thump of his heart, read the question in her upturned gaze and realized the import of what he'd just done. "What rule is that?" she whispered.

"Sorry." Why didn't she slap his face? Why had she responded to his kiss? Why couldn't he keep his priorities straight around this woman? But those were all questions to be answered later.

Nash lowered her heels to the floor, released her and reached over her shoulder to push open the door. The blast of cold air that swept in instantly chilled his skin and cooled his roiling emotions. He nudged Teresa out the door, taking her hand and moving in front of her to lead her down the sidewalk to the corner of the building, where he paused to peek around and ensure their path was safe. He made certain there were no other unwanted visitors watching the parking lot or searching outside the building before he pulled her into a quick pace beside him. Her short legs had to do double time to keep up with his long strides, but she didn't complain. She clicked the car's remote start and had the doors unlocked when they got there.

"You drive." Although he trusted his skills behind the wheel more than hers, she knew the city. Plus, she was 100 percent while his stamina and reflexes were still iffy. Nash swung open the back door and tossed his bag on the seat, pulling out the scraper to brush snow off the windows while she hurried around and climbed inside. "Get the car warmed up and drive out of here nice and normal so we don't draw any attention to ourselves. We'll make your calls on the road and pick up whatever supplies we need later."

She had a blanket waiting for him when he got in beside her, then backed out of the parking space and shifted into Drive. "Where are we going?"

Breathing hard enough to make his shoulder ache, he pulled the cover up to his chin, partly to mask his face and the gun he set in his lap and partly to reclaim the body heat he'd lost outside. "Turn right. Not too fast. I want to get a look at that car."

Nash pushed the seat all the way back and hunkered down as they passed the parked SUV. He didn't see anyone else inside the vehicle. Possibly, they'd split up to pursue different leads to find him or Teresa. Or the man they'd spotted had been calling in backup and was scouting ahead.

"Do you see him?" she asked, catching him looking into the sideview mirror.

"Just getting the license plate."

"Texas?"

"Local rental."

He heard a throaty gasp, this one far different from

that dreamy little sound she'd made after he'd kissed her. "Nash? Behind us."

She'd turned her head to the mirror on her side of the car. Nash glanced back over the seat and sat up straight. He saw it, too. A second black SUV, pulling out of the parking lot across the street and picking up speed. Closing the gap between them.

Forget stealth. "Get us out of here."

He pushed the blanket aside and loaded a bullet into the firing chamber of his gun. Teresa's sedan picked up a little speed, heading down the winding residential street toward some lake or creek at the bottom of the hill. The driver was talking on his cell. That meant he was reporting to... Nash glanced back to the right to see the first man burst through the front door of Teresa's building and charge straight through the snow toward their position on the street.

The man swapped out his phone for his gun and opened fire.

Thunk. The sedan lurched. "Oh, my God! Is he shooting at us?"

"Faster, Peewee." Nash spared a moment to make sure she hadn't been hit as he rolled down his window. The guy popped off two more shots, which pinged off a parked car as they whizzed past and took out one of her taillights.

Nash stuck his arm out the window and fired a pair of warning shots, forcing the man to dive into the snow. He pushed himself halfway out the window and twisted back to take aim at the SUV speeding up behind them. But there were too many civilian targets to risk a shot. The man with the broom. Kids building a snowman. Parked cars and too many trees messed with his line of sight.

But the other driver had no such compunction. He

pointed a weapon out the driver's-side door and fired wildly at Teresa's car. A lucky shot clipped the trunk, and Teresa screamed. Her car zigzagged through a patch of slush, and chips of ice flew up, biting into Nash's face. He recoiled from the stinging assault, wrenching his shoulder.

His luck was going from bad to worse. A block behind him, the other SUV whipped out of its parking spot and spun in a U-turn to join the chase. Nash dropped back into his seat, swearing in pain and frustration.

They weren't going fast enough. "Floor it!"

He stretched his long leg out and stomped on Teresa's foot, pushing the accelerator to go faster. They hit a bump in the road and sailed into the air for a split second before coming down hard and scraping the undercarriage against the pavement.

"What are you doing?" Teresa bounced against the binding of her seat belt. They were passing newer houses now, fewer trees and cars. The road widened, making them easier targets.

"Turn!"

"At this speed?"

Nash grabbed the wheel and jerked it to the right, keeping his foot on the gas when her instinct was to slow down. "Where's the nearest highway?"

"Not close."

They bounced across a bridge over a frozen lake and hit a roundabout intersection. Ah, hell. They were circling back toward the oncoming SUV! Teresa cursed when she saw the gun leveled at them. But the driver hit the same bump they had and lost his grip on the gun. He quickly pulled both hands back to regain control of his vehicle. But as he slowed, the second SUV picked up speed and passed him.

Nash reached for the steering wheel again. "Get us out of this neighborhood!"

"I've got it." Teresa smacked his hand away and stepped on the accelerator. "I've got it!"

She gripped the wheel in both fists and hunched forward. The car careened away from the roundabout, plowing through a drift and careening off the curb as she sped past a stop sign. "I know where we can lose them."

With oncoming cars pulling to the side and the SUVs in hot pursuit, Nash rebuckled his seat belt and braced his hand against the door as Teresa drove through a neighborhood gate and wheeled the car in a sharp right, then sped up the hill to the north. She honked the horn and flew around a slower vehicle. The two SUVs lost a little more distance when she cut through a corner convenience store lot and came out on a four-lane highway heading east, merging with heavier traffic.

One SUV followed the same path but got stuck a few cars back. The driver darted from lane to lane, trying to get around the cars between them. The second SUV was nowhere to be seen. And by the time they'd doubled back through a massive shopping center parking lot near the intersection of two highways, they'd lost both cars following them.

A few minutes later, they were cruising up and down the snow-covered hills of 40 Highway, matching the flow of traffic. With no sinister pursuers reflected in any mirror, Nash holstered his Smith & Wesson and leaned back against the headrest, taking note of his aching shoulder and the slightly winded cadence of his breathing. That encounter had been too close. He was clearly off his game. Yes, they'd gotten away—for now. But they'd have to ditch this damaged car that the cartel thugs could identify as Teresa's now.

But he'd wait and give her that bit of news after she relaxed the death grip she still had on the wheel. "That's some sweet driving, Peewee."

"Thanks. That was exciting." She glanced across the seat at him. "No. It was terrifying. My heart's still racing. Who were those men?"

Cradling his left arm against his side, Nash reached over the center console to capture a velvety strand of coffee-colored hair that had worked free from her ponytail and smoothed it behind her ear. "Try to stay in the moment, Teresa." He stroked his fingers along the line of her jaw, anxious to soothe the tension there. "Don't worry about the future or the past. Allow yourself a minute to just breathe. The crisis is over. We're safe for now. You did great."

He knew she was finally coming out of fight-or-flight mode when she pulled his hand from her face and gave it a quick squeeze. "You're favoring your shoulder again. Did you pull the stitches?" She waited until he sank back into his seat to crank up the heat. "You're the one who should be relaxing. Pull the blanket over you."

"I think that was just a little too soon for that kind of exercise." He winced at the effort of picking up the blanket from the floorboard. She wanted answers as to why her life was being turned upside down, and he needed to talk this through before fatigue turned his brain to mush. "I'm guessing with bullets flying and a high-speed chase that we're definitely on KCPD's radar now."

"Of course we are. Someone is bound to have gotten a plate number or description of the drivers. They'll report it."

"They'll have your license plate number, too. And somebody we drove past might have even recognized Teresa Rodriguez."

Her lips buzzed with a weary sigh. "I'm going to need a new car, aren't I?"

Nash laughed. "I was going to wait and spring that one on you a little later."

She slowed to turn onto a road that would take them to the interstate. "So what do we do next?" Teresa tapped the console between them when he asked for a pen to write down Thug One's license plate number in his log book. "How are you going to find out who's after you if you're hiding? You're not calling your boss in Houston again, are you?"

Not directly, at any rate. Yesterday he hadn't wanted to call in any favors. But today, with Teresa's life as well as his own on the line, he had no choice. "Do you know a place called the Shamrock Bar?"

She nodded. Her eyes were as glued to the mirrors as his had been, still looking for any signs of the SUVs returning. "It's a cop bar downtown. I've been there several times. But you shouldn't drink alcohol in your condition. And a drink is the last thing I want right now. Especially if I have to drive like that again."

"I'm not thirsty, darlin'. I just need to see the bartender there."

Chapter Eight

Shivering, Teresa paused at the neon shamrock in the front window of the Shamrock Bar and gazed through the glass. Inside, the window was framed with a shiny green garland and the corners had been dusted with that fake white spray snow. She'd been here before for a couple of family gatherings, a few outings with her friends and even on a pleasant-enough date with a detective who worked with AJ. But she'd never gone in specifically looking for a man to invite out to a secret rendezvous in the parking lot.

When she heard a car driving past on the street behind her, she peeked over her shoulder to see if one of the black SUVs from this morning had followed her. But as the blue car bounced over the ruts of grated, packed and melted snow on the pavement, she exhaled a puffy cloud of determination and pushed open the front door.

Jake Lonergan was easy enough to spot. There were only a few customers sipping a beer at the polished walnut bar or eating a sandwich for an early dinner at one of the tables.

Nash's description had been simple. *He'll be the biggest thing in there.*

Teresa pulled off her gloves as the bell above the door chimed behind her. Nash was tall and carried plenty of

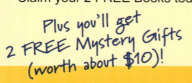

Plus 2 FREE Mystery Gifts!

2 FREE BOOKS

ABSOLUTELY FREE • GUARANTEED

CLAIM YOUR FREE GIFTS

YES! Please send me my **2 FREE BOOKS** and **2 FREE GIFTS**. I understand that, as explained on the back of this card, I am under no obligation to purchase anything!

2 FREE Books

Affix sticker here

M-8801-0792-MG

❏ I prefer the regular-print edition 182/382 HDL GF6X

❏ I prefer the larger-print edition 199/399 HDL GF6X

FIRST NAME

LAST NAME

ADDRESS

APT.#

CITY

STATE/PROV.

ZIP/POSTAL CODE

HI-N14-TF-13

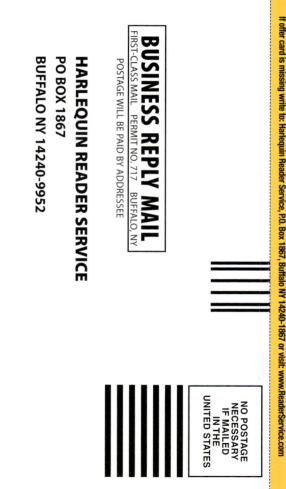

muscle on his lanky frame. From her petite perspective, he was big. But the man setting a stack of crated glasses behind the bar was built like a Mack truck. The silver hair he wore cropped close to his scalp highlighted the scars of a tragic encounter that Nash said had cost the man a good chunk of his memory. If Nash was a wounded bear, then Jake Lonergan was a T. rex with a toothache. Even the green apron and wedding ring he wore did little to soften his beastly appearance.

Definitely the biggest thing in the room. His unsmiling bulk made him the quintessential bouncer who commanded respect and looked as though he could easily handle any customer who dared to step out of line.

And Nash said he was a friend?

Teresa shuddered in nervous anticipation rather than with the cold this time. Her heart rate hadn't been normal since those two men had chased them from her apartment and shot up her car. She needed a nap to ease the stress. She needed to talk with one of her sisters about this emotional pull she felt toward Nash and tell AJ the truth about the man she'd saved, endangered and made a desperate deal with. She needed a chance to rethink some of the choices she'd made in the past twenty-four hours.

Her chance to walk away from Charles Nash and the nightmarish drama he'd brought to her frustratingly sheltered life was staring her right in the face. A public pay phone hung on the recessed wall between the two bathroom doors.

While Nash pulled the tags off the sheepskin-lined coat and gloves they'd bought at a thrift shop and bundled up in the car, she could walk right over there and call 911 or AJ and tell them she'd been kidnapped by an armed stranger. That she'd hidden him in her apartment. That she'd helped him escape from the men pursuing him. That her apartment had probably been ransacked and that two men who worked for a drug cartel had tried to kill her.

They'd tell her to stay put. They'd drop everything and run to her rescue. AJ would put a twenty out on her car and have this place swarming with cops in a matter of minutes. He'd tell the entire department that Nash was armed and dangerous—that he might have harmed his baby sister. There wasn't a cop in the city who would stand by while the family of one of their own was in danger.

Nash would be arrested.

She'd be free of this nightmare.

He'd be taken to a holding cell until he was turned over to a DEA agent who might betray him...or a hit squad found him and finished the job they'd started the day before.

Charles Nash had sworn her life was in as much danger as his.

He'd promised protection in exchange for keeping his secrets and tending his wounds.

He'd kissed her.

Teresa's tongue darted out to touch the rim of her lips. She could still feel him there. The ticklish rasp of his day-old beard against her skin. The firm pressure and unexpected warmth of his slightly crooked mouth molded against hers.

Could she really be feeling something for Nash after knowing him for so short a time? Was this dangerous attraction a lusty response to being forced into the most thrilling adventure of her life? Or was she just as foolish as her brother and sisters claimed because she was so eager to be treated as a useful adult that she mistook Nash's need for her medical assistance and knowledge of the area as some kind of emotional connection?

Should she do this favor for Nash? Or walk over to that phone and call her family? Did she do what she thought was the right thing? Or did she do the safe thing?

"Can I help you, ma'am?" The muscle man behind the bar was talking to her.

Teresa snapped her attention away from her thoughts and focused on the icy-blue eyes watching her. Decision made. She inhaled a steadying breath. She was Nash's partner, not his captive. She didn't need to escape. She didn't want to leave him to face his enemies on his own. She didn't have to understand what she was feeling right now, either. She just had to do what was necessary to keep them both alive.

Her family was going to lock her away in a tower and throw away the key. But not yet.

Teresa threw back her hood, unzipped the top of her coat and crossed the bar to carry out her mission.

"Mr. Lonergan?" She stepped up on the brass railing beneath the bar stools to erase a fraction of the difference between their heights and thrust her arm over the top of the bar. "I'm Teresa Rodriguez."

Jake eyed her hand but didn't immediately take it. "Ms. Rodriguez. I've seen you around. You any relation to Detective AJ Rodriguez?"

"He's my brother."

He nodded as if the familial connection made her presence acceptable and finally shook her hand. "How's he doin'? I don't see him in here much now that he's got those boys to raise."

"AJ's fine. I just saw my nephews this morning. The whole family is well. I'm actually here to talk to you about another friend of yours." She glanced at the lush sitting closest to her, his chin propped in his hand, his leering stare indicating he would have liked to make her acquaintance, too.

But a sharp look from Jake, and the young man turned his curiosity up to the television hanging over the end of the bar.

Jake pulled a towel from his apron and a glass from the top crate to dry it. "I don't have that many friends."

"This one's an old friend from Houston." Jake set the glass on a shelf below the bar and reached for another one, his expression revealing nothing but polite patience. She hurried to recount the message Nash had given her. "He said to tell you that he's the only man from your past who cares that you don't remember him."

That earned her a chuckle. "Charlie Nash."

"You *do* know him." She smiled with relief that he understood the coded message. "He said to tell you he knows you're not in the business anymore, but he's working something big and needs to call in a favor from you."

"Nash is here in K.C.?" She shushed him when the man watching television glanced their way again. Jake dropped his gruff voice to almost a whisper. "How'd you hook up with him?"

"You want to hook up with me, sweetheart?" came a slurred offer from beside her. "I'll buy you a drink."

Another silent warning from Jake and the dark-haired man pulled a ten-dollar bill from his shirt pocket and slapped it on the bar beside his empty glass. "I guess that's a no. I'll be leaving now, Miss Teresa Rodriguez. Merry Christmas."

The man trilled all the *r*s in Teresa's name and the greeting as if the sound amused him before staggering to his feet. He made an effort to straighten his tie before picking up the long wool coat he'd draped over the stool beside him.

"You need me to call you a cab, mister?" Jake offered.

"I'm good." The tipsy man shrugged into his coat and started slipping his buttons into the wrong holes. He pointed to Jake and winked at Teresa. "Not as good as you're doing, pal. But I'm good."

Wondering if this unsettled feeling would plague her anytime a man with dark brown hair showed too much interest in her now, Teresa waited for the drunk to stumble out the door and turn his collar up against the Arctic blast. He was huddled against the front window, punching in a number on his cell phone, when she faced Jake again.

"That was weird." She tried to laugh off the awkward discomfort she felt. "Sober, that guy might be halfway attractive if you go for the preppy type. Drunk, he's just creepy."

"I thought I knew everybody who came into this place," Jake groused, indicating the nosy flirt was as much a stranger to him as he was to her. "I hope he's calling for a ride out there." He stowed the glass and dragged his attention back to Teresa. "Where is Nash?"

"In my car. He doesn't want anyone to know he's in Kansas City. Well, someone does know who shouldn't, but…" She silenced her nervous rambling and matched Jake's direct approach. "Will you come talk to him?"

Jake nodded, understanding this was a serious, as well as secretive, request. "Let me get Robbie in here to cover for me. I'll be right back."

Once Jake exited through the swinging door behind the bar, Teresa perched on a green vinyl stool and glanced furtively around her, wondering if any of the other patrons were paying as much attention to her as that man with the long coat had. The two women in the booth across the way didn't seem to notice her. They were more interested in the two hotties shooting pool nearby. Once

Teresa saw the badge hanging from a chain around one of their necks, she realized they were probably both cops.

Oh, great. Even if they weren't on duty, they might still have been given a description of Nash or even her and her car. Turning her attention back to the door where Jake had gone, she pulled the hood of her coat around her neck and tucked her chin to her chest, hoping none of them knew AJ well enough to recognize her. When the bell over the door rang behind her, indicating more customers, possibly more cops, she hunched down even farther, willing Jake to hurry back out and help her.

She heard a low-pitched drawl behind her instead. "It's me, Peewee. Don't jump."

She startled anyway at the arm that slid behind her back. She spun on her seat to face Nash as he settled on the stool beside her. "What are you doing here?" she whispered in a mild panic. "I thought you were hiding in the car where no one could see you." At least he'd had the sense to turn up the collar of his bulky coat. She reached up to pull the red-and-gold knit cap he wore farther down over his forehead. "You shouldn't be here. Those men at the pool table are cops. What if there's a description out and they recognize you?"

He captured her hand against his warm cheek to mask his face. "You were taking too long. I got worried."

"That drunk was bothering me. But Jake sent him on his way."

"What drunk?" Nash raised his head, scanning the bar, his posture instantly on alert.

But Teresa quickly framed his jaw with both hands and pulled his focus back to her before he drew any-one's attention. "That man by the front window with the misbuttoned coat…" When she glanced over at the shamrock sign and Christmas decorations, she saw nothing through the glass except for a few cars driving past. "Where did he go?"

"I didn't see anyone out front." Nash straightened, concern lining his features.

"Just look at me, okay?" She pulled his chin back to her again. "I don't want anyone to see you."

He leaned in and they touched foreheads, his golden eyes looking right down into hers. "Not a hardship for me, darlin'."

In fact, he spread his knees and moved closer, resting a foot on either side of her stool and sliding a possessive hand along her thigh, turning her efforts to hide him into what probably looked like a lovers' embrace to any curious eyes that might be watching.

It certainly felt like an embrace. She wasn't sure if it was the compliment that warmed her, his protective posture or the levity he used to try to lessen her worry that made her actually feel like smiling. "Maybe the drunk who hit on me caught a cab. I guess he freaked me out a little bit because of those other two men shooting at us."

"Hit on you?" Nash's eyes narrowed above hers. He pulled away a fraction of an inch. "Was something off about this guy? Did he scare you?"

"All he did was offer to buy me a drink. Said my name in a funny way. Like I said, Jake got rid of him." She pushed Nash's stocking cap back from his temple to finger his short thick hair. "I guess I'm only going to be able to trust blonds and redheads now."

"Let's make it just one blond in particular for the next day or so, okay?"

Teresa heard the faintly possessive admonition but was frowning as she felt the dampness in his hair. There was more warmth to his skin than the pseudo embrace could account for, too. "Your fever's getting worse. How are you feeling?"

Before he could evade her question, the door behind the bar swung open. Jake Lonergan entered, followed by an older man with curly black hair and a bushy beard.

"Charlie Nash." Instead of putting on the coat he'd brought with him, Jake reached across the bar to her patient. "You look like hell."

"I'm still better lookin' than you," Nash teased, standing up to shake hands with Jake.

Teresa rose, too, pressing the back of her knuckles against his ashy skin to gauge the warmth there. "He needs to go to the hospital, but he won't listen to me."

Apparently, none of these men were going to. Jake introduced them both to the bar's owner, Robbie Nichols, a robust man who spoke with a lilting Irish brogue. "You go with your friends, Jake. I'll take care of things here."

Really? She wasn't here just to look pretty and be taken care of. Hadn't she put her life on the line, too? Hadn't she lied to her family and taken a huge risk on a man she barely knew? These men might have a few survival skills she lacked, but she had knowledge and training neither one possessed. She tugged at the sleeve of Nash's jacket and insisted he look at her. "You need to listen to me."

"Later. We need to get out of sight first." Nash covered her hand with his and nodded, at least acknowledging her concern before turning his attention to Jake. "You got a place we can talk?"

Robbie was the one who nodded and pointed to the door behind him. "Use my office. No one will bother you there."

"Thanks, Robbie. This way." Jake went to the end of the bar and lifted the hinged gate for them to pass through as the owner picked up a towel to dry the glasses Jake had brought out earlier.

Fine. There was more than one way to handle a recalcitrant patient. If Nash wouldn't listen to reason, then she could do the bullying thing herself. Teresa asked the older man for a lemon-lime soda with lots of ice before Nash scooted her into the back hallway. Jake locked the office door behind them and offered them guest chairs. Nash sat in the closest one, his strength clearly flagging. While the two men talked about Agent Nash's desperate situation, Teresa opened her backpack on the corner of the desk and dug out a bottle of aspirin.

She recognized the small black notebook Nash pulled from inside his coat. She'd gotten herself into hot water that morning by reading through his secret names and cryptic notes and had possibly made it necessary for them to go on the run. Whatever the names and numbers in there meant, clearly it was of vital importance.

"This is everything I've been able to put together on this case." Nash held up the notebook. "Three days ago in Houston, I must have asked the wrong question of the wrong person. Next thing I know, my apartment's been trashed, my confidential informant inside the Graciela cartel says their chief, Berto Graciela, knows I'm a cop and he's put a hit out on me. I had two other agents, Axel Torres and Jim Richter—you don't remember them, but we've all worked together in the past—inside different arms of the organization, as well. They were both exposed as undercover agents and murdered last week."

Teresa's stomach twisted into a knot at the revelation of such tragic events. Nash had lost men he worked with—friends, most likely—to the senseless violence of the drug trade. He must have been aching with grief and guilt, and yet the two men talked as if conducting a business meeting.

"How can I help?" Jake asked, thumbing through the notebook Nash handed him. "You know these names don't mean anything to me anymore. My amnesia wiped the slate clean—until I dealt with that hit man the Gracielas sent after me."

"Yeah, you did a good job of disrupting business there for a while when you took out old Diego Graciela." Nash grinned, although his humor never reached his eyes. "We were having pretty good luck working inside the organization and taking advantage of the power struggle between Berto and Diego's lieutenant, Santiago Vargas. It's easy to funnel intelligence in and out when one side doesn't know or trust what the other's doing. That all ended last week when my men started dying."

Jake tapped one of the pages in the notebook. "And these starred names are your suspects as to who leaked your identities to the cartel?"

"Oh, my God." Teresa felt the blood drain from her head to her toes. She sank onto the corner of the desk beside her bag. "I thought the stars meant those people were important to you. That they were the good guys. I'm so sorry."

"It's okay." He reached over to squeeze her hand. "You didn't know. I'd have tried the same thing if I'd been in your shoes. Maybe if I'd told you the truth instead of tying you up, you wouldn't have contacted Puente."

Jake arched a silvery eyebrow at that last exchange. "Umm...?"

Nash released Teresa and waved aside any curious questions about the rocky start to his partnership with her. "Let's just say we've had some trust issues."

"So what's the deal with you two?" Jake asked, leaning his hip against a credenza in front of the frosted-glass window. "Teresa's no agent. And it's not like you to get someone involved who isn't trained for the job."

"No, it's not," Nash agreed. "But I need her." He un-snapped the top buttons of his shirt and pushed it back to reveal the bandage covering the wound on his shoulder. "I figure a hospital is the first place the DEA and the cartel will look for me."

Teresa saw a small dot of red seeping through the gauze. "I should change that dressing."

"Later."

"Later you'll be dead if you don't let me do my job." She peeled back the tape to look at his injury.

He smoothed the bandage back into place. "Peewee?"

She propped her fists at her hips. "Nash?"

Jake interrupted the dueling wills. "I heard about the shoot-out at the chop shop on the news. The reporter said it was gang related."

Nash snapped the front of his shirt, effectively brushing aside her usefulness. "Not any local gang. They were cartel men. And there are at least two more in town still after me." He glanced up at Teresa. At least he had the good grace to stamp an apology on his chiseled features. "After both of us." He returned to his conversation with Jake. "That reminds me. Can you get your hands on a local police report? See if there was a break-in reported at Teresa's apartment? Find out if anything was damaged or taken." His gaze ping-ponged back to her. "I want to buy you a new phone, get your car fixed for you and repay you for any damages to your home."

"You're the only thing damaged in my life. Here. Take these and drink all this. Your body needs the electrolytes." She held out two aspirin and the lemon-lime soda. When he shifted in his chair to continue his conversation with Jake, Teresa shifted, too. "Now, Nash. You asked me to take care of your injuries and keep you alive. I can't do that if you won't let me help."

Jake chuckled behind her. "Now I get it. She's tough enough to go toe-to-toe with you. Sounds like a lady I'd listen to." Teresa turned and nodded her appreciation for his support once Nash had swallowed the pills and taken a few sips of the drink. "So she keeps you alive. What do you need from me?"

"Information. I don't know who to trust back in Houston, so I can't call for backup. I need you to run a couple of local license plate numbers—see if the rental agreement gives me a name I can run down."

Jake nodded. "I've got a connection I trust at KCPD. He knows how to be discreet. I'll give him a call."

"I know I'm asking a lot. I've already lost three men on my team."

"I used to be on your team before this." Jake pointed to the scar at his temple. "You were the only one who ever bothered to try and find me when everyone else gave me up for dead. You helped me fill in the blanks of my memory so I was free to marry Beth and make a life here in K.C. I owe you."

Brushing aside his friend's avowal of loyalty and gratitude, Nash picked up a notepad off the desk and started copying down some names and numbers from his black book. "I know you don't remember Captain Puente—the guy we reported to at the Houston office—"

"I've heard you mention his name. He was our boss on undercover ops. You want me to try and reach him?"

"I wouldn't," Teresa cautioned, regretting the mistake she'd made that morning.

But Nash seemed to have it all figured out. He tore off the top sheet of paper and handed it to Jake. "I want you to call every name on that list, not just the captain. Even though we'll be alerting the mole, it should also alert anybody else who's on our side. Maybe you'll get a feel for whoever is hiding something." He snatched the paper back and wrote another name. "I want you to ask about Tommy Delvecchio, too."

"The agent who got killed here in K.C.?"

Nash nodded. "Let me know that his body got back to Houston okay. And any funeral arrangements if they got 'em. The number for my disposable cell is at the bottom. I don't know if he was seeing anyone, but his parents are both alive. I want his family to know that he died doing his job."

Jake folded up the paper and pocketed it in his jeans. "It'll take me some time to make the calls to get the information you need. You got a place to stay? My home is on an acreage. It's pretty remote—"

"No." Using the armrest to brace himself, Nash stood. "I saw a nondescript place that won't ask too many questions when we were picking up supplies. We can crash there for a few nights. We'll be fine. You've got a little girl and a baby on the way. These guys have had pretty good luck tracking me. I'm not going to bring a gun battle to your home."

Was that twist on Jake's mouth a smile? "Wouldn't be the first time."

She'd probably just imagined his morbid idea of humor. The scars that both men bore indicated a sad familiarity with violence. Yet, like her brother, it hadn't stopped them from standing up to the bad guys and protecting what they believed in—their city, their homes, the people they cared about.

Teresa packed her bag and zipped her coat, feeling woefully inadequate to be a part of their quest for justice for their fallen friends. At the very least, she would not be a burden to their investigation. And she would not be the source of any more trouble. "I'm ready to go whenever you are, Nash."

His golden-brown gaze dropped down to hers. "I know you are." He reached for her hand and laced their fingers together, pulling her to his side as he faced Jake. "This one's ready for anything. I wouldn't be here without her."

Had he read her mind? Had he sensed her second-guessing her place in this partnership? Whatever the reason for his words of praise and tactile show of support, the simple gesture warmed her, reassured her. It felt good to be needed. It felt better to hear Nash admit how much he needed her. *Her.* As though she could handle the job. As though she was enough.

She could do this. They could do this. Together.

"What about wheels?" Jake asked, his presence reminding her that her relationship with Nash was all about protection and medical treatment and finding out the truth. It wasn't about the way Nash forced her to be stronger, smarter, more stubborn—the capable adult she'd always known she could be. He hadn't babied her. Not once.

No wonder she kept thinking she was falling for him. He treated her the way she wished her family would treat her. Like a grown woman. She'd never had anyone like that in her life before. If she wasn't careful, she really would fall in love with Charlie Nash.

Nash's fingers reached for hers when she pulled away, but she wisely pulled her gloves from her pockets and kept both hands busy putting them on. If Nash noticed her sudden withdrawal, he didn't let on.

Neither did Jake. "You're going to need a vehicle that can't be tied to either one of you. Here." He pulled a key from his wallet and tossed it to Nash. "Take my truck.

It's the silver pickup behind the bar. There's a gun in the glove compartment, if you need it."

Nash thanked him. "I've got a go bag. We'll be fine."

After checking to make sure the hallway was clear, Jake shrugged into his coat and escorted them down the hallway to the bar's rear exit. "I'll find out what I can and call you tonight on the burner phone." Hunching his big shoulders against the evening chill that dampened the air and hinted at another dusting of snow later on, he led them out to the silver pickup truck parked near the Dumpster. "The gas tank is full. I'll get a ride from Beth after work."

The two men retrieved Nash's bag from her car and stowed it in the back of the extended truck cab. They exchanged a few more private words before shaking hands one more time. "Thanks, Jake. Call as soon as you know something."

"I will." And then the big man nodded to Teresa. "Ma'am. You take care of this guy. He's the oldest friend I can remember. Take care of yourself, too."

"I will. Thank you."

After Jake strode back inside the bar, Nash opened the driver's-side door and handed her the key. "You'd better drive."

He made sure she was settled behind the wheel of the big four-wheel-drive truck before he circled around and climbed into the passenger seat beside her.

Once more, she and Nash were outside in the cold, alone again.

Chapter Nine

The Seaside Motel wasn't much of a tropical oasis in the wintry urban sprawl of Kansas City, Missouri. The "sea" was a cracked concrete pool filled with drifts of snow and two plastic palm trees chained to a peeling wrought-iron fence. The "motel" included two single-story buildings arranged in a U shape with the office around the empty pool. Twelve chipped and dented steel doors faced their own parking spaces.

The old man at the front desk who checked them in had a flask behind the counter, a reality show on his portable TV and not so much as a curiously raised eyebrow for Nash when he registered as Mr. and Mrs. John Smith and paid an extra twenty dollars in cash.

He had to give the owner credit for trying to upgrade the place by lining the porchlike overhang with colored Christmas lights. Some blinked, some didn't. And every so often along the way, a bulb was burned out, broken or missing. Each door was draped with tattered fake greenery studded with red plastic berries. Teresa fingered one of the sprigs of plastic holly as Nash unlocked the door to 6A.

"Festive, huh?" he teased before pushing open the door and turning on the lights.

The musty smell of disuse greeted them inside. Teresa

dropped her backpack on one bouncy mattress and his go bag on the other while he locked the door and pocketed the key. Then she pulled back the velour bedspread and sniffed one of the pillows. "At least the sheets are clean. They've been bleached."

Great, so no bedbugs. Still, it wasn't the kind of place he'd ever want to take a woman like Teresa. In this kind of weather, he pictured them in a cozy lodge with big throw pillows and a thick wool blanket on the floor in front of a stone hearth. Sipping cold beers, warming themselves by the fire, getting better acquainted. Him exploring those curves. Her putting those soft, firm hands on him. The two of them getting *very* well acquainted.

Nash swallowed hard, scratching his parched throat, quickly burying wherever that fantasy had been headed. Teresa had shed her coat and was already running water in the sink and checking out the bathroom when he apologized. "Sorry it's not the Ritz."

"It's not like we have much choice," she answered through the door. "Your friend Jake said those men went through my apartment."

He'd already gotten the first of what he hoped to be several informative reports from Jake Lonergan. Unfortunately, learning her place had been broken into and searched wasn't exactly the positive news he'd been hoping for. "Yeah. Sorry about that, too. I don't think we left anything behind that could tell them where we are, but they know we're together, they know I'm alive, and they won't stop hunting for us."

"Thank you for letting me call AJ to tell him I'm all right. I'm sure he'd still prefer to see me in person to tell him that, but—"

"That's not going to happen. It's hard enough to stay

hidden from Graciela's men. I can't have half of KCPD looking for us, too."

"I know." The toilet flushed and she reappeared. "I told him I'm staying with a friend for a few days. That'll just have to hold him until we're done with your mission."

"A friend?" He hardly qualified. Maybe she was getting a little too good at telling lies.

"Don't worry. I have a lot of friends. Even if he does check up on me, it'll take him a while to contact all of them." She stuck her fingers under the tap to wash her hands. "I'm mostly mad that those men damaged some of the presents I'd gotten for my nephews and the kids at the hospital. I'll have to replace those before the twenty-fifth."

"I'll replace them," Nash insisted, hoping the traitor in his office would be exposed and he'd be alive to celebrate Christmas. As fatigued as he was, he was determined to stand tall on his own two feet and show her he could protect her. "It's my fault your place was violated by those scum. You send me a bill for whatever replacing the lock and door costs, and let me know how much I need to reimburse you for your patients' gifts or anything else they ruined."

She shut off the water and reached for a thin white towel. When she was done drying her hands, she turned and chucked the towel at his head. "You're doing it again, Nash. All this talk about tabulating expenses and reimbursing me makes me feel like the hired help. That's not the mutual partnership I agreed to."

"I'm not used to needing anyone but the men I work with, Peewee." Nash caught the towel and tossed it onto the bed. "I'm not quite sure how I'm supposed to deal with you."

"How did you deal with the team you worked with in

Houston?" She walked straight across the room to him and started unbuttoning his coat. Despite the professional efficiency of her fingers, having her undress him felt a little too intimate for his waning self-control around her.

"Not like this." When she started to push his coat off his shoulders, Nash caught her by the wrists and pulled her hands away. But he wasn't strong enough to let her go, and with a surrendering sigh, he pulled her right up to his chest, winding his arms behind her back and tucking his chin atop the crown of her hair. "I want to take care of you, but you don't want to be taken care of."

She snuggled inside the opening of his coat, her fingers clinging to the front of his shirt. "Did you try to 'take care' of your men? Or did you let them do the job they were trained to do?"

"Both," he answered honestly. "Richter, Torres and Delvecchio were like little brothers to me. On one hand, I knew they were good agents—I trained Jim and Axel myself. On the other hand, they were my responsibility." His arms convulsed around her, and he dipped his head to bury his nose in the fragrant softness of her hair, clinging to the present as the grief and guilt of the past few days surged through him. "I did a real whiz-bang job of taking care of them."

"Charlie, don't."

"Charlie, hmm?" He shouldn't have liked her calling him by the given name nobody used as much as he did.

"None of this is your fault. That's what you told me, right?" Her arms snuck around his waist beneath his coat, and she turned her cheek into his shoulder. "None of it." She found where his spine met his belt with her fingertips and dug them in, pulling herself into his embrace. Her breasts pillowed against his chest. Her hips rubbed against his. Her cheek rested over the thump of his heart. "Does this hurt?"

He knew she was talking about the bruising, stitches and bullet hole in his shoulder. But all he noticed was the way her warmth and energy seemed to wrap around him and seep into every cell of his body, easing some of the emotional pain and making even those most beat-up parts of him hum with an awareness of her feminine strength. "Not a bit."

"It's like I tell my patients when they have to go in for another treatment or operation. Don't judge the future by your past. Yes, horrible things happen." Her fingers drummed a nervous pattern against his back before linking together and tightening her hold around his waist. "My father was murdered when I was little—I barely remember him. My mother died of cancer early last year. I got mugged walking home from my first job after high school. The guy gave me a black eye and stole my purse and probably sentenced me to forever being the Rodriguez that everyone else has to look out for."

Nash rubbed slow circles up and down her back, surprised to learn that she'd had to endure such tragedies. "If you're trying to make me feel better, I have to tell you that all you're doing is pissing me off. I hate that you had to go through all that." He slipped one hand up to the nape of her neck, tunneling his fingers beneath her thick ponytail and massaging the tension he found there. "And now I've gotten you involved with this mess? I'm the one who's trouble."

She laughed at his grousing, sending warm vibrations through his body. She turned her lips to his chest and pressed a kiss to the swell of his pectoral through his cotton shirts before snuggling in again. "But good things happen, too. There are more patients who get well than who never make it out of the hospital. AJ finally arrested the man responsible for my father's death. I miss my mama, Sofia, but I have so many wonderful memories of her." She loosened her grip at his back and leaned back against his arms, tilting her face up to his. "You'll get this guy. We'll stay two or three steps ahead of those gorillas he works with, and you'll get him. I know you will."

The spicy scent of Teresa's skin and hair filled his head with every breath. As much as he loved the feel of her diminutive curves clinging to the length of his body, he loved her spirit even more.

Nash lifted a strand of coffee-colored hair that had fallen across her cheek and rolled the soft silk between his thumb and forefinger. "You just don't know how to quit, do you?"

"Nope."

He unwound the hair behind her ear. He smoothed aside another strand and tucked it behind the other ear. He stood head and shoulders above her, framing her face between his hands, looking down at those dark eyes and that beautiful mouth.

Then she pushed up onto her toes, and he lowered his head and they were kissing. Not that sweetly tentative introduction they'd shared at her apartment building. This was twenty-four hours of pent-up desire and battling wills and raw desperation breaking free in a meeting of mouths and tongues and gaspy moans.

Teresa's lips parted in welcome, giving him a taste of her utter softness and fiery warmth. Her hands braced at his waist. His fingers slid into her beautiful hair, tangling, sifting, holding on as her tongue danced with his. He traced a path along the smooth line of her jaw with his lips, then worked his way back, dropping a dozen little nibbles along the way. He nipped at the decadent curve of her bottom lip, and she murmured his name in a sound that was heady pleasure to his ears. He touched his tongue to the spot and felt her lips tugging at his, urging him to deepen the kiss again.

When Nash obliged, she skimmed her hands up the planes of his chest, caught his rough face between her hands and rubbed her palms against his beard stubble, creating a passionate friction. And then her arms were snaking around his neck, her hands were in his hair.

He fell back against the door, and she came with him, her toes leaving the floor as he palmed her butt and took her weight against his chest. His pulse thundered in his ears. His body burned. Her nipples beaded beneath her sweater, poking him like delectable hot brands. He wanted his hands on her breasts. He wanted his mouth there.

This was all kinds of crazy. All kinds of stupid. All kinds of right.

Her thigh wedged between his, her arms tightened around him, and she sort of crawled up his body, her eager gasps and clinging hands tempting him to forget everything except the perfect storm of this moment. But even as anticipation leaped behind his zipper, Nash's energy short-circuited. He was crashing.

Of all the lousy luck.

He wanted this sexy little spitfire in ways beyond what his body was craving. But if he was going to make love to this woman, he damn sure wanted to do it right. He wanted to make sure he could follow through and give her everything she wanted. Everything she deserved.

And she deserved a lot better than the one-night stand in this seedy dump of a motel that he could offer her. She deserved her family and Christmas and a guarantee that being with him wouldn't get her killed.

Nash tore his mouth from hers and nuzzled the softness of her hair, dragging in ragged breaths beside her
ear. "Darlin', I'm sorry."

Her breath gusted across his cheek. "What's wrong?"
Her lips scudded across the same spot. "I'm not complain-
ing. This pull that I feel toward you doesn't make any
sense, but I wanted you to really kiss me. I wanted..." She
stiffened in his arms. She pushed his chin away from her
ear and leaned back to read his face. "Nash?"

The hand squeezing her bottom and the one palming
the bare skin of her back tried to hold on when she began
to slide back down his body. "I'm so sorry."

She braced her hands against his chest and pushed
to free herself. Nash flinched at the stab of pressure
against his bum shoulder. His left hand popped open
and he dropped her.

As soon as her feet hit the floor, she was at his side,
sliding beneath his right arm and walking him to the
closest bed. "You're white as a ghost. I'm such an idiot."

"No." He squeezed her shoulder, glad that she didn't
have to carry his weight like the night before but appre-
ciating the balance she offered. "The mind is willing, but
the body just isn't up to doing this tonight."

He sank onto the edge of the bed, and she immediately felt for his temperature. "I'm the one who's sorry."
She reached around him to help him remove his heavy
coat without lifting his left arm. "I got carried away by
my hormones and the stress of the past couple of days. I
wasn't even thinking."

"That makes two of us."

She tossed his coat onto the chair beside hers and went
to work on the snaps of his shirt to get to the wound. "But
I should know better."

That stung worse than the blow his male ego was already dealing with. He grabbed her wrists and stopped her halfway down the placket. "And I'm such a lowlife taking advantage of the woman I kidnapped that I don't?"

Her mouth was still pink and swollen from the passion they'd shared. But the argument for trust remained. "I thought we were beyond that, Nash."

He liked *Charlie* better coming from her, but going back to trading barbs with Teresa was the splash of reality he needed. He released her and let her tend to him. "Right. We're partners. But trust me, none of my team ever tempted me to forget a mission the way you do."

She paused with her hands at the hem of his T-shirt. "I'm on a mission, too." Her sure hands weren't quite so efficient as she peeled off his T and inspected the entry and exit wounds she'd stitched up. Then she retrieved her backpack and set out the medical supplies they'd purchased. She put on a pair of disposable sterile gloves, unwrapped a gauze pad and soaked it with distilled water. "You need me to be a nurse. I'm determined to do my job and do it well. I'm so tired of not being allowed to do the things I'm capable of, of not being trusted to make good decisions. And then when I sabotage myself—"

"By making out with a randy cowboy cop from Texas?"

A soft smile finally relaxed her mouth. "My brother and sisters would call for an intervention if I told them that."

"They don't picture you with a bad boy like me, huh?"

"On some days, I don't think they picture me with anybody. Unless he's staid, boring and unlikely to ever put his hands on me." He gritted his teeth as she gently cleansed his mending skin. Yeah, that keeping his hands to himself would definitely cut him from the family approval list. "They don't trust me to make the best choice in men or where I live or—" she shook her head "—who I stop to help along the side of the road."

Nash turned so she could clean and dry the stitches in his back. "I think I understand where your family is coming from. You're lucky that someone cares enough to worry about your safety and happiness."

"Your team was like that for you, weren't they," she deduced. "They were your family, and you guys cared about each other—like brothers, you said. No wonder you're so determined to get the man responsible for their deaths."

He nodded and faced her again while she opened a tube of antibiotic ointment. She didn't have anything in that bag that could fix the wounds inside his head and heart. But there was something about the woman herself that seemed to find those hurting places inside him. She exposed them—probed deeper into a few, gently tended others and, somehow, made him feel a little better.

No wonder he was so drawn to her. He really did need her. Maybe more than he'd ever needed anyone his whole life. If she thought for one moment that he didn't know just how lucky he was to have her with him in this nightmare, then he needed to make that right.

"Teresa..." He reached out to pull down the hem of her sweater, which his groping hands had bunched up around her waist. "I'm trying to do the right thing here. Not just by my men but by you, too. I may not be the smoothest guy on the planet. But I do know how to treat a lady right. I can't tell you how much I want you. But this is the wrong time, wrong place—I may even be the wrong man." Her hands stilled their work and rested on his shoulder. "I can't offer you much of a future. I may not even be able to offer you next week. You deserve better than that."

She nudged aside his knee and stepped between his legs, winding her arms around his neck in a hug. "So do you, Nash."

His arms encircled her waist, and he rubbed his cheek against hers. "Yeah, well, I just want you to know that I'm grateful you're here with me."

They held each other like that for several endless moments, her legs butting against the bed, her chest pressed to his, her strong, tender arms holding him close as she gently rocked him in her embrace. The sting of tears made his eyes feel gritty, but he refused to shed them. Grief, guilt and regret tore through him just as violently as those two bullets had. He'd been in survival mode for far too long. This ornery, petite, strong, irresistible woman had forced him into human mode. It hurt to care about the people he'd lost. It scared him to think about everything he could still lose.

He buried his face against her neck and held on to her healing compassion for just as long as she'd let him.

A BING CROSBY holiday tune played softly through the static of the AM station Teresa had found on the radio. Other than the twenty-four-hour Christmas music playing in the background, it was silent as Nash polished off a sandwich and two cups of Teresa's chicken noodle soup while they sat on the edges of their respective beds, facing each other.

Part of his current aversion to conversation was savoring just how filling and delicious her food tasted, even under these crude conditions. Part of it was the nagging feeling that he really was growing weaker by the minute and wouldn't be able to keep watch over her the way he'd promised. And part of it was his wayward thoughts, which kept reliving that kiss and imagining where it would have ended up if he was a whole man—imagining where this deep, unexpected bond he had with this woman could lead if he didn't have a crooked cop and at least two cartel thugs breathing down his neck.

Not even the late hour or the flyaway strands of dark hair that had pulled loose from her ponytail throughout the day could diminish her beautiful Latin vitality. Realizing he'd been staring, he blinked and looked away.

But she had his number and was on her feet in an instant. "You look like you're about to fall asleep."

She took his empty cup and paper napkin in one hand and pressed the other to his forehead and cheek. He was sorry that touching him made her frown like that. He was sorrier when she moved away, taking her homey kitchen scent and her soft, firm touches with her. She set the trash on the table beside the thermos and reached into her bag. "I'm going to give you another aspirin, and then I'm putting you to bed. Sleep is what your body needs most right now." She spun around and snapped her fingers. "And an ice pack."

She took a sharp turn from the trash can to grab her coat and headed for the door.

"Wait." Nash pushed to his feet and caught her by the arm before she reached the door. "You can't leave. It's dark out there. You won't be able to see if anyone's following you."

"I'm just going down to the office to get some ice. If I'd thought of it sooner, I'd have gone when we first arrived." She nudged him, encouraging him to sit back down. When he refused to move, she patted his arm. "There are lights on each of the buildings and streetlamps out front. I'll be there and back before you even miss me. Unless you'd rather go to the hospital?"

"Nicely played, Peewee." Nash covered her hand with

his. "Okay. I'm not getting much better on my own. We'll risk the ice run."

While she zipped her coat and put on her gloves, Nash pulled his gun and went to the window. He peered out through the drapes. What was it, maybe twenty, thirty yards to the office door? When she stood beside him with the ice bucket, he looked through the peephole to make sure things were quiet in every direction before he turned out the interior lights and opened the door. "I'll watch you from here. Go straight down the sidewalk and back. Don't speak to anybody. If you're out of my sight for more than twenty seconds, I'm coming after you."

"You could be resting while I'm gone," she suggested.

"It's not a negotiation."

"What else is new? I'll be quick." She flattened her palm at the center of his chest, maybe thanking him for the little taste of freedom, maybe reassuring him that she'd be back, before she turned around and hurried away.

Nash grinned as she power walked those short legs beneath the glow of the Christmas lights hanging from the gutters. Lurking in the darkness of the doorway, with his gun down at his right thigh, hidden from view of any-one outside, he counted how many rooms at the motel were occupied and familiarized himself with the vehicles parked there. There were two pickups with ladders and gear boxes that probably belonged to construction workers or a road crew. There was a tank of an old sedan with some kind of medals hanging from ribbons on the rearview mirror. There was what he assumed was the manager's car parked in front of the office and a sporty little muscle car caked with ice and road grime that had come from Colorado.

But there were no black SUVs cruising past on the street. He saw no one peeking through a window blind to follow Teresa's movements or note him standing in the shadows beneath 6A's plastic garland.

He couldn't believe how good the brisk night air felt on his face and in his lungs—until he started to shiver with the chills. He knew he should go get his coat, but he wasn't about to leave his post. Still, the moment the office's glass door swung shut behind Teresa, Nash sagged against the doorjamb and exhaled a puffy cloud of breath in the frigid air.

Maybe he should let her call her brother again and have her request protection from the vaunted Detective AJ. Her family had to be going out of their minds with worry if they knew about the shoot-out near her apartment. If he felt this weak, this weary, he wasn't going to be any good to her, much less capable of going toe-to-toe with a traitor.

And if anything happened to Teresa because of his failing, he might as well be a dead man.

Nash's cell phone rang, and he straightened against the door frame again to pull it from his pocket. Since only one person had this number, he had no qualms about answering. "Hey, Jake. What do you got for me?"

Jake Lonergan might not have remembered his life as a DEA agent, but he sure remembered how to give a mission brief. "Made all your calls. Everyone in the Houston office knows you're alive and knows you're in the wind. Captain Puente says he and a Cruz Moreno have already booked a flight into KCI Airport tonight. They asked for your contact info. Both said it was vital that you get in touch with them if I hear from you again."

Nash trusted that Jake hadn't given him away. "Did they give you a hard time?"

"They both pumped me for info on your location and condition, but I wasn't in a talkative mood."

Stubborn cuss. The Jake he knew had never been much of a talker. "What else?"

"Puente confirmed that the Gracielas have men in the area."

"That's not news. Did he say how many?"

"He wasn't sure. He thinks even Berto Graciela himself is en route to find you. Sounds as if Santiago Vargas maligned Berto's name, saying he had no business leading the cartel if he didn't even know he had DEA agents working for him."

Nash checked the time and started counting down the seconds until Teresa needed to reappear at the office door. "Vargas has no room to talk. He didn't know, either. Not until Puente or Moreno or whoever it was sold us out."

"Captain Puente said Vargas hasn't been seen for a couple of days. There's no word of any hit on him going down, either."

"What are you saying?"

"What if Vargas is in K.C., too?"

"Both of them? Here?" He almost laughed. So who was back home running the drug-smuggling business?

"What better way to show the cartel who really gets the job done than by serving up your head on a silver platter?"

Nash swore under his breath. Didn't that just make a man's day? Knowing two ruthless drug-lord wannabes and a potential army of well-armed thugs had joined him here in Kansas City for a deadly reunion? "What did they say about Tommy Delvecchio?"

"No details yet. Apparently, there's some kind of holdup at the medical examiner's office with the bodies from the warehouse. Neither Puente nor Moreno could tell me what the problem was. I can ask Spencer to look into it."

A pulse of light bounced off the palm trees by the pool, drawing Nash's gaze. A car must have turned the corner and was coming down the street toward the motel. "Is that your friend at KCPD? Did you talk to him?"

"Yeah. Spencer Montgomery. That conversation went about as well as you thought it would."

"Tell me."

"He says that AJ Rodriguez is personally investigating the break-in at Teresa's apartment. I don't think he bought her story about staying with a friend for a few nights."

Just what he didn't need. A big brother with a beef and a badge. "Does he know if AJ has figured out anything?" he asked.

"Not yet." Jake's answer wasn't reassuring. "But Spencer said AJ worked several years on a drug task force, doing undercover work. He knows all the same tricks you do. If anyone is going to piece together what's going on, it's Rodriguez."

"Ah, hell." That wasn't just any car coming down the street. It was a black-and-white unit from KCPD. No lights flashing, no sirens blaring. But it was pulling into the Seaside's parking lot.

"Nash?"

He pulled back into the darkness of the room and closed the door, leaving just a few inches open to see out. His toes tapped anxiously inside his boots as the squad car pulled into the parking space right beside the manager's car. Nash's gaze shot over the two uniformed officers climbing out of the vehicle to the office door. *"Teresa?"*

"Talk to me," Jake urged, understanding that something had put Nash on alert.

"We may have company. Keep me posted. Talk to you later." Nash disconnected the call and jammed the cell into his pocket. The need to take action, to dash across the parking lot to get her out of there, jolted through his legs. "Come on, darlin'."

There she was. She appeared in the glass doorway, pushed it open. Nash's breath locked in his chest. But she never made it out the door. One of the officers said something to her and pointed back inside the office. Her gaze breezed past Nash's position before the officer's bulky frame blocked her from view.

Nash's pulse kicked up a notch. What the hell was going on? Had they been discovered? Had that slimy manager somehow recognized Teresa from a news story or description her brother had put over the wire and called it in for some kind of reward? While the first uniformed cop ushered Teresa back inside the office, the other pulled back the front of his coat and braced his hands on either side of the utility belt at his waist, scanning the motel and parking lot. Nash quietly closed the door and moved to the window to watch the office and cops through the drapes.

The second officer left his position at the black-and-white and walked toward building A. Nash glanced back at his go bag. What if these weren't cops at all? What if the mole had somehow gotten wind of the vehicle switch they'd made at the Shamrock Bar and reported Nash for auto theft and marked him as a fugitive? He could arm himself to the teeth and take both men out. But there'd be a lot of witnesses, maybe even a few innocent bystanders who'd get hurt.

Nah, if they'd come for him, he'd surrender peacefully. He'd take his chances in lockup. No way was he going to put Teresa's life in more danger than he already had.

The cop batted at some of the Christmas decorations when he stepped up to the first door. But as he strolled down the sidewalk, Nash could see there was noth-

ing nonchalant about his purpose here. The older officer glanced at the license plates of the two construction
trucks. When he stopped in front of Jake's silver pickup,
Nash pulled back from the window and flattened his
back against the wall, waiting for the knock at the door.

Thirty seconds, maybe a minute, passed before Nash
heard the man's boots on the cold concrete. Once he was
certain the cop was moving on, Nash returned to the
window to see him walking on to building B. Was that
a misdirection to get him to drop his guard and reveal
himself? Or were the officers looking for someone else?

Wouldn't that just be his luck? Nash eased out a tense
breath, beginning to suspect the latter, when the officer
circled around the white Impala with the ribbons hanging from the mirror. Then he turned his mouth to his
shoulder to report something on his radio—probably to
his partner.

Raised voices and movement at the opposite end of the
motel pulled Nash's gaze back to the office. The first blue
suit was coming out of the office, holding Teresa and the
manager both by the elbow. The young man released her
and exchanged a few words. The complaints were coming from the gray-haired manager, whom the officer had
handcuffed. "Come on, darlin', get out of there."

But Teresa stood there hugging the ice bucket and
shivering in the cold while the cop put the old man in
the backseat of the cruiser. Her gaze came straight to
6A, even paused at the window as if she could see him
there—asking him what to do, perhaps warning him.

The young officer slammed the car door, startling her.
When she whipped her head around, he said something
to dismiss her and she scuttled out of the way. While she
stepped onto the sidewalk, the young cop jogged straight
across the parking lot.

He ran past Jake's truck as Nash heard pounding on another door. The first cop announced himself as KCPD and ordered the occupant to open up. In the midst of shouts and protests, Teresa approached their room. But to his surprise, she walked on past, not letting the uniformed officers know her destination, not giving him away.

She was well past 2B when the officers dragged two half-dressed teenagers out the door. They put them both into the Impala with some serious kind of lecture, because the lanky boy kept putting his hands up in the air instead of starting the car. Once the engine was running and the kid was nodding yes to everything the older cop was saying, the younger cop went back to their black-and-white. He picked up his partner and they followed the teens out of the parking lot.

As soon as the drama left the Seaside Motel parking lot, Teresa ran back to the room.

Nash was there to open the door before she could knock. He pulled her inside and locked it behind her. "What the hell?"

She set the bucket on the table beside the door and paced the length of the room and back. "Apparently, Mr. Moscatelli rented one of his rooms to a pair of minors. At first the officer said they were looking for a couple who hadn't registered under their real names. He asked me if I'd seen anyone."

Hence taking her back inside the office. "Did he threaten you in any way? Did he seem suspicious of you?"

"No. I don't think so." Man, she was pale beneath the cold red apples on her cheeks. Whatever had happened had scared her. "The manager pointed to us in the registry, but then Officer Britt got a message from his partner about a license plate and he told me to get back to my room. I thought they were coming for you. For us."

Nash holstered his gun and stopped her when she turned to pace away again. "They were here to escort those teenagers home. The police probably got a call from a concerned parent."

Teresa nodded. "Officer Britt's partner said something about finding 'the boyfriend's' license plate number."

So they'd tracked the kid's car. "Did the officers recognize you?"

"I don't think so." She was visibly shaking as she unzipped her coat. "I didn't know either one of them."

"Did they ask for your name?"

"Yes. Teresa Smith. Right?"

Relief warred with pride. Nash palmed the back of her neck and kissed her, hard and quick, thanking her for being smart enough to think on her feet and protect them both from discovery. "Thank you, Mrs. Smith."

As quickly as she smiled at his praise, her forehead knotted with concern. "You didn't need another stressor like that. Get to bed before you fall over." She shushed him when he started to protest. "I need you healthy, okay?"

He nodded, feeling the clammy chills that had probably alarmed her. "Okay."

In five minutes flat, she'd given him another aspirin, removed his boots and pulled the blanket and bedspread over him. She made an ice pack out of one of the hand towels and placed it on his forehead.

As warmth and fatigue rushed up to claim him, he pulled away the ice pack and sat up. "You don't open that door for anybody, understand? Don't answer the phone if it rings. Don't call anyone. Don't give anybody any reason to know that we're here."

"Yes, sir." She nudged him back down to the pillow and put the towel back in place.

"I'm trying to protect you. I'm about to pass out for a few hours. I need to know you'll do exactly what I tell you so I know you'll be safe."

She pulled the bedspread off her bed and tucked the extra layer of warmth around his shivering form. "I will. Is it all right if I keep the radio playing until I fall asleep?"

He nodded, wondering if she'd slipped him some kind of sleeping pill or if he really was too exhausted to stay tough with her. He hadn't listened to any Christmas music this season, hadn't thought much at all about the holidays until he was hiding in this dump with this woman who was starting to mean a lot more to him than a nursemaid should.

He pushed himself up on one elbow before sleep could claim him. He reached for the Smith & Wesson on the shelf between the beds. "Do you know how to fire a gun?"

"Yes." She pushed his hand away from the gun and covered him up again. "AJ showed me. He's taken me to the firing range a couple of times. He wanted us all to understand gun safety since he kept one in the house. But I don't like using them. I've dealt with more than one gunshot victim in the children's ward."

"Still, if it's a choice between dying and shooting someone, I want you to—"

"I'll wake you up."

He nodded, surprised at her trust. He sank back into the pillow, praying he could live up to that trust. "Don't leave me, Peewee."

"I won't."

"Don't be all clever and brave...." Man, his eyelids were heavy. "It's not safe out there."

"I'm here to take care of you, remember?"

Yeah. She'd promised to stay. He wouldn't lose her. He wouldn't lose anyone else. "Good night, Peewee."

"Good night, Nash."

She was still watching over him when he drifted off to sleep.

Chapter Ten

"Nash." Teresa tugged the covers tangling around his long, writhing legs and leaned over him to touch his burning face. "Nash, wake up. We're going to the hospital."

When she'd awakened to the sounds of his heartbreaking moans and the bed rattling against the wall, Teresa hadn't been sure if Nash was caught in the throes of a nightmare or delirious from fever. Probably some combination of both. But if he kept twisting around in the bed like this, he'd rip his stitches. And then she'd have a whole new possibility for infection to worry about.

Fear sharpened her decision and made her reactions quick. She'd already fished the keys from his coat pocket, loaded his bag in the truck and started the engine to warm up the cab. There was no negotiating this particular difference of opinion anymore, either.

She gave his cheek a firmer pat. "Come on, cowboy. Wake up."

"Teresa?" She barely got a glimpse of golden-brown eyes before he grabbed her by the shoulders and pulled her down onto the bed beside him. He pushed the hood off her head and ran his fingers over her hair, dropping kisses onto her forehead, her nose, her mouth before he wrapped her up in a suffocating hug. "I couldn't get to you. They had you and I couldn't get to you."

Teresa held on for a few precious seconds, then wedged her elbows between them to push away. "It was a bad dream. I'm right here. I'm real. I'm fine."

"I don't want to lose you."

When he reached for her again, she rolled away off the far side of the bed. "You can't get rid of me now, partner."

The focus in his eyes was still half-blurred with sleep when he sat up. "You should have just told them what they wanted to know."

"Told who?" She pulled his legs over the edge of the bed and knelt in front of him to tug on his boots.

"Berto Graciela and his men. They had you and..." He caught her face between his hands and tipped it up to see the agony lining his. "Don't let them hurt you. I'm not worth it."

A surge of anger fired through her blood that he'd think that. She grabbed his wrists and stood. Even if he was a tad delirious, she still argued with him. "Don't you ever say that, Charlie Nash. Your men are counting on you. I'm counting on you. We're going to get through this." As her words sank in, he slowly nodded. "Now get on your feet. You're coming with me."

While he tucked his shirttails into his jeans, she picked up his gun from the bedside shelf, checked the safety and opened up her backpack. But a big hand closed over hers and the gun before she could place it inside. Nash rose unsteadily beside her, taking the weapon from her grasp. "Not your job."

He holstered the gun at his belt. She fetched his coat and helped him into it. She stretched up on tiptoe to pull the red-and-gold stocking cap over his head. And then they stumbled out the door into the dim morning light.

After loading him into the passenger seat of the truck, Teresa paused for a moment, looking for any signs of activity or curious eyes around them. But the sun was barely an orange glow peeking over the horizon. It didn't look as though anyone else was up yet. Besides the blinking Christmas lights, the only glimmer of any kind of movement besides them was the strobing effect of the television someone was watching in the office, although the different car parked near the door made her think someone else had come to finish out Mr. Moscatelli's shift.

Convinced their departure remained undetected, Teresa climbed into the truck and buckled up. She spared a few moments to rub her fingers together in front of the heat vent to get some feeling back into them.

"I'm okay, Peewee."

"No, you're not."

"I know. I'm in a bad way." He reached over and folded his hand around hers, offering a warmth and reassurance that were in short supply this morning. "I mean, I was having a nightmare before. I couldn't shake some of the images. But I'm not losing it. I promise."

She shifted her grip to lace their fingers together and squeeze his hand before pulling away. "Good. You're hard enough to handle when you do make sense." That earned her an echo of that crooked grin. She checked her mirrors and shifted the truck into Reverse. "I'm still taking you to the hospital."

As she pulled into the street, he leaned back into his seat. "If anything happens, I want you to—"

"Nothing's going to happen." She watched the cars pulling in behind her, as much to see if she recognized any black SUVs as to note the beginnings of rush-hour traffic filling up the streets. Once she was on the six lanes of interstate heading south, she pushed her speed, knowing she had to get across the city to one hospital in particular. "I know people I can call in favors from, too. I've got a way to sneak you in."

"I'll make a fugitive out of you yet."

Teresa glanced over to smile at the teasing remark. But his eyes were closed and his handsome mouth was pressed into a tight line of pain. She moved her seat forward another half an inch and put more pressure on the accelerator.

Dr. Emilia Rodriguez-Grant got very quiet when her temper was brewing. Instead of giving Teresa the order, she nodded to her sister to inject the syringe of antibiotics into Nash's exposed hip. His answering grunt was the loudest noise for the past five minutes in the silent E.R. bay at the Truman Medical Center.

"You actually did a good job with the stitches," Emilia announced, her tone nothing but that of one medical professional to another. "And the wound track looks clean."

Teresa disposed of the syringe in the sharps receptacle while Nash pulled up his shorts and refastened his jeans. Emilia picked up the gauze and tape from the rolling supply tray beside the examination table and re-covered Nash's wounds, carefully avoiding jostling the IV needle and tube attached to the back of his hand.

"I can do that," Teresa offered, knowing a trauma nurse usually took over for the E.R. doctor at this point anyway.

But Emilia was focused solely on Nash, completely unintimidated by his towering height or the fact she had to stand on a step stool beside the exam table to address his injuries. She met his probing gaze while she worked, chatting with him as though he was any other patient who'd come into her emergency room—instead of one who'd bypassed most of the check-in paperwork and been sequestered immediately inside a curtained-off trauma bay.

"I replaced the cotton stitches beneath the skin with degradable sutures," Emilia explained. "The biggest part of your discomfort is from the muscle tear in your shoulder. But that should heal itself with time if you let it rest and don't strain it with repetitive motion. The X-ray doesn't show any bone fragments besides the tiny one I removed. That should ease any of the sharp pain you had in your shoulder. You're lucky that bullet didn't ricochet in the other direction and nick your lung or your heart. Or else even my resourceful baby sister here wouldn't have been able to save you."

"Yes, ma'am. Real lucky." Her dark eyes narrowed, as if judging the sincerity of his humble agreement. Teresa's gaze bounced from one to the other, trying to figure out to what degree her sister resented doing this favor for her—and what retribution it would require to make up for it.

"I've ordered you a prescription for antibiotics." Emilia was back in efficient work mode again. "That spike in temperature could be attributed to a combination of dehydration and blood loss. The IV fluids seem to be bringing it down. I don't detect any signs of infection, but the pills are precautionary when you have a foreign object like that rip through your body. Do you want painkillers, too?" Nash's silent glare was answer enough. "No, I don't suppose a man like you would."

She set the remains of the tape onto the tray, then turned atop the step stool, rubbing both her back and belly simultaneously, indicating the toll this eighth month of pregnancy and demanding workload was taking on her body. When she leaned over to brace her hand on the bed to step down, Nash's hand was there. For a moment, Teresa thought her sister might stubbornly refuse the offer to help.

But she took Nash's hand, accepting his support only long enough to get both feet on the floor before quickly pulling away. "Thank you."

"Thank you, Dr. Grant."

Emilia nodded, accepting some kind of détente with him. But she wasn't quite ready to deal with her sister yet.

"Emilia—"

"We finish with the patient first." Emilia peeled off her sterile gloves, nodding to Teresa as she walked past. "Then you and I need to talk."

Fine. While her sister tossed her gloves into the trash and jotted something onto Nash's chart, Teresa climbed up on the same step stool to pull the hospital gown hanging at the crook of his elbows back over his shoulders before tying it loosely around his neck. "I sent your shirts up to your room. You can re-dress as soon as the IV is done and we take it out. I told the orderly to move you to room 3010. Standard procedure is to keep someone with an injury like yours overnight for observation."

"I can't do that, Peewee. We can't stay in one place that long. Especially a location as public as this."

"For a few hours, at least."

Emilia lifted her observant gaze from the clasped fingers between Teresa and Nash. "Thirty ten is in the children's ward."

Teresa let go and stepped down. "I know that part of the hospital better than any other. I'll recognize if anyone or anything is out of place there. I can watch over him and *I* won't look out of place."

She tucked the stool back into the closet cabinet where it had come from while Nash eased to his feet. "I still vote for getting out of here."

Teresa was holding firm on her original plan. "You promised me a few hours here. You have to stay until that IV is finished. And what if you need a blood transfusion? Or more fluids? I snuck you into this place once. If you have a relapse, I don't think I'll be able to do it again without raising even more suspicion."

There was a soft knock at the open door beyond the curtain. Teresa peeked through the drape before pulling it aside and letting the bald orderly pushing a wheelchair enter. "The patient's ready. Would you take Mr. Smith up to 3010."

The dark-skinned man arched a nonexistent eyebrow. "The children's ward?"

She walked Nash to the wheelchair, rolling the IV stand along with him, dismissing the orderly's confusion with a smooth lie. "He wants to be near his daughter."

Nash halted beside her, dipping his head to her ear before sitting. "Do you know him?"

Teresa smiled, helping him into the chair and covering him with a heated blanket. "I can vouch for Chester. He's worked here longer than I have. I went to high school with his daughter." She squeezed Nash's hand and sent him on his way. "I'll be right up." She gave directions to the orderly that weren't on the chart. "It's a private room, Chester. I don't want him startling any of the kids up there, so close the door."

"Will do." Chester unlocked the wheels, hooked the chart over the back of the chair and rolled him toward the door. "Okay, sir. I'll make this ride as smooth as I can."

"Teresa—"

"I know." She stopped Nash's warning by pulling the blanket up past his chin to mask his face a little. "If I'm not up there soon, you'll come looking for me."

He nodded, then pulled down the blanket and shifted his gaze to Emilia. "Don't blame her."

"I don't." Emilia was waiting for an explanation after Teresa closed the door and pulled the curtain. "Really? Sneaking a wounded agent into my E.R.? Is he why someone broke into your apartment and trashed it? Justin said there were reports of gunfire in your neighborhood. Did he have something to do with that, too?" Teresa didn't have to answer the barrage of accusations. Emilia was already shaking her head, turning away. *"Madre de Dios."*

"You can't tell AJ."

"You may have become a pretty little liar over the past few days, but I haven't." Emilia rolled the tray over to the counter and sorted items into trash and what could be stored away for use. "You know the hospital is mandated to report gunshot and stabbing victims to the police."

"Couldn't you lose his paperwork for a day or two?"

"Teresa." Emilia pulled out a metal stool and sank onto it, already tired on a shift that was only a few hours old. "Has he brainwashed you? Now he's got you thinking like one of them."

"One of *them*?" Teresa's shoulders stiffened at the insult. "He's not a criminal."

"He's not John Smith, either. Are you sure his badge is real?"

"Yes. Try not to stress any more than you have to. I'm worried about your blood pressure." Teresa advised her sister to stay put and took over cleaning up the supplies for her. "I told you, Nash is an undercover DEA agent. The man who set him up to be murdered is a fellow cop. He didn't have anyone he could trust. He asked for my help. What would you do?"

"I'd call Justin." Her husband the cop. "Or AJ."

"But Nash thinks the agent who betrayed him in Houston is covering up the fact that he's a cop so that KCPD will treat him like a fugitive from the law." She stowed the last of the supplies before facing her sister. "The cartel has far-reaching influence, Emilia. Nash said that if he goes to jail, there'll be someone there to kill him."

"How do you know you can trust him? Do you believe everything he says?" Emilia's eyes narrowed, then widened as if she'd just discovered something in Teresa's expressions. Maybe something more than the utter trust she had for Charles Nash. "Oh, *Gamberro,* no. You don't think you're in love with him, do you?"

Was that what this feeling was? This gut-wrenching fear that she could lose him that clouded every decision? The fiery desire that made the passion she'd felt for any other man pale by comparison? That curious instinct that made her believe she knew Charles Nash better in three short days than she knew any other man?

"I don't think it," she finally answered.

Emilia shook her head. "And he's put you in that kind of danger?"

"He's protected me at every turn."

"And what kind of future does he promise you?"

"He doesn't." The sorrow that gripped Teresa's heart at that notion proved the depth of her feelings for the man. "I imagine that once he finds out who set him up and has that man arrested, he'll go back to Houston. To his job, to his life there. But right now he needs me, Emilia. Like no one has ever needed me before." Teresa circled the room, finally making sense of why Charles Nash meant so much to her. "He needs me to be strong and capable. He lets me do things. He lets me argue with him. I don't feel like the baby of the family when I'm with him. I just… I feel like…me. He lets me be me."

Emilia reached for her hand across the stainless-stee

counter, perhaps understanding more than Teresa had given her credit for. "When I first met Justin, I thought he was a criminal. When I found out he was an undercover cop, he was still just as dangerous. It's not an easy life."

Teresa squeezed her sister's hand, unused to hearing this cautionary tale about her marriage. "But you looked past the danger. You got to know the man he was underneath that bad-guy persona. Justin is a good man. You love him."

"With all my heart." Emilia's serene smile warmed with the love she was used to seeing there. "Justin saved my life."

"I remember the bomb threats around the city that year. He saved me, too."

"He's a wonderful husband and a good father. And now we're having our second child together." Emilia released her hand to cradle her swollen belly in a maternal hug. "I'll keep your secret. I'll list the patient as John Smith and send the bill to you—with the promise that he pays you for it, like he said."

Tears stung her eyes as Teresa smiled her gratitude. "He will. Nash is a stickler for repaying a debt and keeping his promises."

Emilia stood, slipping back into doctor mode for a moment. "He'll need his dressings changed once a day for a couple of days. After that, he'll need air to get to the wounds for them to heal properly. If there's any green or yellow discharge, he'll need to come back and see me."

"I know the drill." Teresa pulled her sister into a hug. "Thank you. For taking care of Nash—and for giving me the chance to take care of him."

"Don't make me regret this." When Emilia pulled away, her eyes were a little bright, as well. "If anything goes wrong…if you get hurt—"

"I know a good doctor."

"I don't just mean physically. If you care for him, and he—"

"I know a good friend, too." She hugged her again before gathering up their coats and her bag and heading out the door. "I love you."

"I love you, too." Teresa was halfway to the elevators when she heard her sister groan. "What are we going to tell AJ?"

THE HOSPITAL WAS swarming with cops.

Okay, so maybe *swarming* was a bit of an overstatement. But the black-haired man with the graying temples and wrinkled suit striding down the hallway carried himself with an air of authority like law enforcement. The uniformed KCPD officer walking beside him confirmed it.

Teresa ducked back into the hospital gift shop, hugging the bag of clothes she'd just bought for herself and Nash. She pretended a rapt interest in a display of Kansas City postcards as the two men entered the gift shop and crossed to the clerk at the counter to introduce themselves.

The dark-haired man pulled out his badge and clipped it onto the pocket of his suit jacket. "Good afternoon, ma'am. I'm Jesse Puente, an agent with the Drug Enforcement Administration. This is Officer Reynaldo from your local police. We're looking for someone."

That man was Nash's supervising officer? The captain she'd inadvertently alerted to Nash's location when she'd sent him that frightened email? Panic jumbled her thoughts for a moment. What should she do? Nash was only two floors above them. How had Puente and the other officer tracked him here to the hospital?

Go. Run. No. Don't draw attention to yourself. Just mosey on out of here, then beat it upstairs to warn Nash.

The conversation faded as Teresa shifted the package in her arms and headed into the hallway. But the glass door hadn't closed behind her before Captain Puente called out to her. "Teresa? Teresa Rodriguez?"

She kept walking. She wasn't in scrubs today, wasn't wearing her name badge or classification pin since she was off the clock. For all anyone knew, she was a guest here to visit a sick friend.

"Ms. Rodriguez?"

When he asked the clerk for confirmation of her name, Teresa knew she had no choice but to stop and face the two officers hurrying down the hall behind her. "Yes?"

The older man was all smiles as he slowed his pace and approached. "Hi, I'm Captain Puente. We exchanged emails?"

"Ma'am." Officer Reynaldo looked bored with introductions and more interested in watching everyone who entered the hospital's main lobby and came down this corridor to the gift shop or visitor elevators at the end of the hall.

She shook the captain's hand when he offered it. "Nice to meet you."

If he noticed any reticence in her greeting, he didn't respond to it. "In your email to me, you mentioned you were a nurse. But you didn't mention where you worked. Some of my men from Houston and your local PD are checking out area hospitals, searching for Agent Nash. It's lucky I ran into you."

"Yes." She moved her sack behind her back, hiding the men's shirt and underwear she'd just purchased. "Lucky coincidence."

"Do you mind if I ask you a few questions?"

Teresa shook her head. She minded like crazy, but if she could keep the cops occupied down here on the first floor and maybe even send them on their way, then they wouldn't find Nash upstairs.

"This is where you work?" he asked, probably confused by her sweater and jeans. "You're out of uniform."

"Yes. I'm off duty today. Doing a little Christmas shopping. We get a discount here."

"I'm glad that Agent Nash has released you. He's no longer holding you against your will?" So much for pleasantries.

Something down the hallway caught Officer Reynaldo's attention and he circled around behind her. Teresa clenched her toes inside her boots to keep from bolting. Even though they'd effectively blocked her escape in either direction, he still didn't seem that interested in her, so she tilted her gaze back to the older man and concentrated on Puente. If Nash wasn't sure he could trust him, then neither was she. "No. As you can see, I'm a free woman. I was never in any real danger. It was just a…miscommunication."

Puente pulled back the edges of his jacket, giving her a clear look at the gun he carried as he rested his hands at his waist. "I was hoping you'd call me so I could reach Nash. I've lost three agents already. I don't want to lose another one."

His paternally indulgent tone made her suspicious instead of putting her at ease as he'd most likely intended. "Some men broke into my apartment. Looking for Mr. Nash, I expect."

"You weren't hurt in the break-in, were you?"

She was getting too good at this twisting-the-truth-into-a-lie thing. "I wasn't there at the time, but I haven't wanted to go back to check my computer or anything else on the premises. And I didn't have your number."

He arched a black eyebrow. "You can't check your email from another location?"

"I've been very busy."

"Excuse me, sir." Officer Reynaldo came up behind Teresa, and she stiffened. But the brief whiff of the tacos or burritos he'd had for lunch quickly receded as he backed away again. "There's a good view of the parking lot across from the elevators. I thought I'd go take a look."

Puente nodded, dismissing him. "I'll be back in a few minutes. You can show me around the rest of the hospital then."

The rest of the hospital?

A nervous suspicion shimmied down her spine. "How many of your officers did you say were here, Captain?"

"I didn't." He folded his hand around Teresa's arm and pulled her aside, ostensibly to clear a path for the balloons-and-wheelchair entourage coming down the hallway with a new mother and baby. But he didn't release her. "I get the idea you don't trust me, Ms. Rodriguez. I want to help you. I want to help Nash. But I need information. Where is he? How is he? Look, I get that he's threatened you to keep his secrets."

Teresa twisted her elbow from his grasp. "He hasn't threatened me. I'm not afraid of him."

"He's probably told you, then, that if we can connect you to him, then the Graciela cartel can, too." He braced a hand against the wall and leaned toward her. "Graciela's men are here in Kansas City. They want Agent Nash. I suspect they're the ones who broke into your apartment. They'll use you to get to him. I've seen the Gracielas' torture victims. Most of them would rather be dead."

She tightened her grip around her backpack and the

sack. "Stop trying to scare me. Nash explained how dangerous the men after him are. Why do you think I'm avoiding my apartment?"

Puente grinned, dropping his hand and pulling away. "So at least I know he's alive. And nearby, I'm guessing."

"All I did was patch him up. I haven't seen him recently." At least that, technically, wasn't a lie. She'd been hunting down clean clothes that would fit him for the past half hour. "He was injured in the shoot-out where your Agent Delvecchio got killed."

His dark eyes narrowed. "What do you know about Tommy?"

"Only what Nash—Agent Nash—mentioned when I was helping him. He said Agent Delvecchio was like a kid brother to him." She glimpsed movement behind her from the corner of her eye. Officer Reynaldo. Had there really been anything to look at outside? Or were the two men cornering her into a trap? Teresa's breath stuttered in her chest. "Maybe you all felt that way. I'm sorry for your loss."

He shrugged. "We're still looking into Delvecchio's disappearance. Thank you."

"Wait." Something wasn't right. "You said disappearance?"

For a moment, Jesse Puente looked grim. But just as quickly, that pleasant professional facade reappeared. "Apparently, the M.E.'s office here in Kansas City isn't releasing the bodies from the warehouse to us, pending identification."

"Sir?" She startled at Reynaldo's voice beside her. "I just got a call that the main office has the E.R. record for the past few days you were asking for."

"Good." Captain Puente pulled out his wallet and handed her his card. "If you see Nash again, have him call me. He may not trust anyone right now, but I can help him. But not if the cartel finds him first. If he needs backup, tell him I'm closer than he thinks."

Teresa accepted the card, a little surprised to see Puente already retreating down the hall after Officer Reynaldo. "You're letting me go?"

He paused. "This is just a friendly conversation, Ms. Rodriguez. I'm not detaining you in any way. This is a big city. And I'm not that familiar with it. It's hard to find someone under those conditions. Especially when he doesn't want to be found."

And yet Puente had found her.

"It's my job to follow up on any leads. And you're the best one I've had so far. But as you said, you've had no further contact with Nash. So I have no reason to take up any more of your time. *Gracias.*"

Teresa didn't realize she'd been holding her breath until the captain caught up with Officer Reynaldo, and the two men fell into step and crossed the lobby toward the business offices.

Then her lungs emptied with such a rush of relief that it left her light-headed. She swayed against the wall for support. But only for a few seconds.

The moment Puente and Reynaldo disappeared around a corner, Teresa spun around and hurried toward the elevators. But five steps and she stopped.

She glanced back over her shoulder to see if either officer or anyone else was watching her. The hospital lobby was busy. The gift shop had the clerk and a handful of customers inside. Although Puente and Reynaldo hadn't reappeared, there were too many people to keep track of. She needed to make sure no one followed her up to the third floor.

Instead of heading for the elevators, she changed

course and opened the door to the first empty consultation room she passed. With one last peek over her shoulder for curious eyes, she closed the door and cut through the room's back exit into the hospital employee area. She hurried through a break room and came out in an inner hallway, away from anyone's watchful eyes. Once the coast was clear, she dashed over to the employee elevator and got in to go to the third floor to find Nash.

Chapter Eleven

"Nash?" Teresa pushed open the door to 3010 and darted inside.

"That was too long, Peewee."

She butted the door shut and tossed him the bag of clothing. Nash was sitting up on the edge of the bed and caught it with his good hand. He dumped the contents onto the bed and ripped open bags and tore off tags with an urgent sureness that made her think he was feeling stronger.

"I know. Sorry."

"Tell me what's happening." His dirty-gold hair stuck up in rumpled spikes on one side of his head, as though he'd just awakened from a nap. But he'd already pulled on those big scuffed boots and had his gun strapped to his belt. Shirtless and golden, bruised and bandaged, her wounded bear seemed to have found the energy for one more battle.

"Your captain is here. In the hospital." Teresa dropped Jesse Puente's card on the bed as she hurried past to open the tall slim cabinet that functioned as a closet. She pulled out their coats. "He wants you to call him. He said he could help you and offer backup if you need it."

"He showed you his badge? You're certain it was him?"

She nodded, stopping at the bed to stuff her own change of clothes into her backpack. "There was another man with him. He wore a local uniform, but he kind of gave me the willies. He wasn't paying attention to the conversation. He was just…lurking."

He pulled a T-shirt over his head. "Did you catch a name?"

"Officer Reynaldo. Does that mean anything to you? Is he in your little black book?" Nash squeezed her shoulder as he shook his head. "Puente said he had a whole team of officers and agents combing the city looking for you."

He pulled the IV from his hand and shucked into his shirt. "They're not going to find us. Let's go."

Grabbing their coats in one hand and her arm in the other, Nash peeked into the hallway before opening the door. "Which way?"

She pointed to the right. "Back stairs are down there."

Clinging close to the wall, keeping his head bowed but his gaze on a constant scan, he led her down the pristine white hallway. Three steps. Four. Five. She plowed into his back when Nash suddenly stopped and swore beneath his breath. "Moreno."

He snatched her hand and quickly reversed course.

"What is it?"

"Company."

She glanced back to see the two men at the counter of the ward's central desk. Although they had their backs to her, it was easy to recognize a uniformed police officer. But she guessed it was the man with the cowboy hat and curly black hair Nash wanted to avoid. "Do you know him?"

"Yeah." He ducked into the first room on the left, pulling Teresa in behind him. "*He's* in the book."

Her stomach knotted. A cartel man or the suspected mole. Right here. In her hospital. Not twenty feet from where Nash was peering through the slit he'd left open in the doorway. Teresa fisted her hand in the back of his shirt, willing him to put more distance between them and the people who wanted him dead.

Nash retreated, all right. But only to urge her to move. "Hide our stuff."

Teresa turned. Froze. She hadn't checked the room number. "Oh, no."

Laila Alvarez was propped up against the pillows in her bed, playing with her stuffed horse. She smiled. "Hey, Mr. Nash."

"Hello again."

"Again? Mr. Nash?" She couldn't stop him from brushing past her and pulling aside the middle curtain to make sure the second bed in the room was empty. "You two know each other?"

He closed the curtain and opened the closet, pausing for a moment to assess its size. "We've met. Hide our gear."

"Hey, sweetie." She spared a reassuring smile for Laila before following him to the cabinet closet, where he was pulling out hangers and tossing them into a drawer. "We can't stay here and endanger a patient."

"We can't go out there."

"But—"

"Every person in this hospital could be in danger if one of Graciela's men decides to take a shot at me." He grabbed their coats and stuffed them into the drawers, too. "If we get out of here, the danger comes with us. Now hide."

"I hate this. How do you two know each other?" She opened another drawer and set her backpack inside.

"I took a walk as soon as Chester left me in the room. I needed a better idea of exits and who belonged here and who didn't." He winked at the girl in the bed. "We talked about Texas for a couple of minutes."

"You were supposed to be resting—"

Nash pressed his finger over her mouth and shushed her. "Moreno's coming this way. Get in."

"There's no room for both of us, you big beanpole." She heard the men's voices approaching, too. "Bend your legs. That's it."

"Teresa—"

She pushed him into the closet and shut the door. She nervously patted her chest to make sure she wasn't wearing any identifying pins or nametags, then pulled up a stool beside the bed. This wasn't much of a plan, but it was the only one she could come up with on a split second's notice. "Laila, I need you to be very brave. Don't tell anyone anything about Mr. Nash. It's like hide-and-seek, and we have to win."

"Okay." Her favorite patient looked small and fragile with her pink knit cap on her bald head and the oxygen clip on her finger.

But her dark eyes lit up with anticipation as Teresa asked for her help. "We're going to play a pretend game now, okay? You be a patient, and I'll be your friend who's come to visit you."

"That's not much of a game."

"You can't call me Teresa. You have to make up a name."

The little girl laughed. "Okay, Laila."

Teresa squeezed the girl's hand as she heard men's voices outside the room. She picked up one of the Marguerite Henry stories stacked beside the bed. "Shall we read a book?"

"You go down that side. I'll check over here." A man's voice preceded the soft knock at the door. It opened without invitation, and the curly-haired cop from Texas strolled in. He stopped when he saw Teresa and pulled back the front of his jacket, flashing both his badge and his holstered gun. "Excuse me, ma'am. Good afternoon. I'm Agent Cruz Moreno, DEA. We're following up on a lead and conducting a search of the hospital."

"What do you think you'll find in this little girl's room?"

He smiled, probably used to charming his way into getting what he wanted. "Mind if I take a quick look around?"

"As a matter of fact, I do. She needs her rest."

Agent Moreno took a couple more steps into the room. "I just need a quick look at that bed behind you, ma'am."

Before Teresa could stand and block his path at the foot of the bed, Laila piped up with one of her curious questions. "Are you a cowboy?"

"Huh?" Cruz Moreno stopped, looking almost startled to hear the patient speak.

"You're wearing cowboy boots and a hat. You're supposed to take it off inside. Do you have a horse?"

"No, kid. I'm a cop." He dismissed Laila and directed his explanation to Teresa. There was no charm to his words or smile now. "I'm looking for a man. Taller than me. Light hair. He may be injured."

Teresa shrugged. "This is a pediatrics ward. We don't have any adult patients here."

"This is my friend Laila," the little girl interjected.

Agent Moreno ignored the introduction and moved toward Teresa. The man wasn't that tall, but he was huskily built, and she got the idea that he was willing to throw some of that weight around. "He might not be a patient.

He might be masquerading as one of the staff or acting like a fugitive."

"What's that?" Laila sat up from her pillows, determined to be heard.

"A criminal. Someone who doesn't want the police to catch him. Seen anyone like that, kid?"

Sensing his irritation, Teresa drew his attention back to her. "I haven't seen anyone like that. Are we safe here?"

"Depends on how desperate he gets. Don't worry, ma'am. We'll find him." His shoulder brushed against Teresa's and she flinched away as he reached around her to pull open the curtain. He chuckled when he saw the empty bed. "I thought maybe you were hiding something from me, Laila."

Teresa held his suspicious dark-eyed gaze, keeping his focus on her and not the closet. But before she could think of the dismissive words that would chase him from the room, the real Laila started talking. "You have an accent. Are you from Mexico? They have horses there. They speak Spanish and Andalusians are Spanish. From Spain. They're horses."

"What?" Agent Moreno shook his head. Laila's questions seemed to confound him. And distract him from his purpose.

"Do you have an Andalusian horse?" she asked.

"No, kid." He tipped his hat to Teresa and slipped past her to the door. "Sorry to have bothered you, ma'am." Teresa's feet stayed rooted into place until the door closed and she heard Moreno talking to the other officer outside. "Without any better leads than what we've got, this is like searching for a needle in a haystack. Let's call this floor clear and start looking where the grown-ups are."

Teresa hurried to the door and peeked through a small

opening just as Nash had, waiting for Moreno and the other officer to get on the elevator at the end of the hall. She looked the other direction, too, seeing no one but a couple of staff members she recognized.

"They're gone," she announced, dashing back into the room. She opened the closet door and crossed over to Laila to give her a gentle hug. "Sweetie, you were wonderful."

"Did we win?"

"You bet we did," Nash answered, sliding out of the cramped space.

Laila was still sitting up straight in the middle of the bed, her dark eyes eagerly following Nash's every move. "I don't like him. He wears fancy cowboy boots. Not real ones you can work in, like yours. His were too shiny." Nash handed Teresa her bag and coat. "I like you. You listen when I talk. Even when I'm boring."

He flashed the girl a crooked grin that had captured Teresa's heart, as well. "I like you, too, darlin'. And somehow I doubt you could ever be boring. I owe you one for helping me out." He slipped into his coat before helping Laila get situated back under her covers. Teresa's breath did funny things in her chest when he leaned over to kiss the girl's cheek. "I won't forget."

Teresa had a kiss for her, too. "Bye, sweetie. You do whatever the doctors tell you, okay? I'll be back for Christmas."

Laila held on to both their hands. "Are you coming to the Christmas party, too, Mr. Nash?"

Golden-brown eyes locked on to Teresa's over the girl's bed. She read the message there. Christmas, even just a few days away, was too far in the future for him to even consider. To even hope for.

Before Teresa could plead with him to move beyond

that fatalistic outlook, he released Laila and started for the door.

"We'll see, darlin'." He clasped Teresa's hand instead, pulling her into step behind him. "Let's get out of here. I assume you know a back way?"

Teresa nodded and moved into the hallway ahead of him. "Follow me. The emergency wing is closest to the garage where we parked."

A nod or a smile to the coworkers they passed was enough to discourage any conversation. Although she imagined there'd be plenty of questions about the tall, tough-looking man following her down the hallway when she came back to work on the twenty-fifth.

Provided she'd be alive and able to report back to work.

The possibility that she might not, that she might lose Charlie Nash even if she did survive, sharpened her gaze and hurried her steps.

No one met them coming or going down the back stairs. They didn't even run into anyone as they jogged through the employees' inner hallway.

But when she opened the door into the busy waiting area down by the E.R., she saw the one thing that could stand in the way of their escape. A cop.

Teresa pulled up and hung back in the stairwell. "Nash, look. With Emilia."

He peeked over her shoulder to watch Emilia and the uniformed officer walking down to the E.R. bays where they'd been that morning. "Do you think she's telling him about me being here?"

"No. She promised."

"Wait a minute. Ah, hell." He tensed behind her. His fingers bit almost painfully into her shoulders. "That gun isn't regulation."

"What difference does that…?" The shiny silver pistol that stuck up out of the officer's holster had meant nothing to her. But when the man chatting with Emilia turned, glancing up and down the hallway, his gaze moving right past the shadowed doorway where they hid, Teresa's knees wobbled, and she leaned back into Nash's grasp. "That's the man who was at my apartment. Why is he dressed like a cop?"

Nash swapped positions with Teresa. He pulled back the front of his coat, checking his own sidearm. "Why do you think?"

"Captain Puente," she groaned. "He called me by name. He knows I work at this hospital."

Nash swore as the fake cop held open one of the swinging doors and followed Emilia inside. "Then he knows your sister does, too. Stay put."

"He won't hurt her, will he?" Nash's answer was to dart across the hall, flattening his back against the wall there. "Where are you—?"

But he was already stealing down the hall and slipping into the E.R. entrance next to the door through which Emilia and the man had disappeared.

Worried now for both Nash and her sister, Teresa followed. She copied the slim profile Nash had used and sidled along the wall until she reached the E.R. doors. Although there were four separate sets of swinging doors along the way, the workstations inside were sectioned off into several more bays divided by privacy curtains. The configuration of the rooms made it easier to change the layout to meet patient needs. Unfortunately, the interior curtains also made it nearly impossible to know where her sister and the cartel thug had gone or where Nash might be. But when she heard the fake cop's thickly accented voice challenging something Emilia had said, Teresa went straight to the doors where their conversation was escalating into an argument.

"Where is your sister and her boyfriend?" the creep demanded.

Teresa peeked through the window. When she saw the curtain was drawn, she pushed the silent door open and sneaked inside to do whatever she could to protect Emilia.

Although the curtain blocked her view, Teresa could hear Emilia moving about the work area with the cool efficiency of the doctor she was. "I have no idea what you're talking about. I told you the E.R. was empty. Now get out of here. You're contaminating this room."

"You don't know how to reach your own sister?"

"She's on vacation from work. It's the holidays."

"You lie."

Teresa dropped to her knees at Emilia's startled yelp. Her blood ran cold when she peeked beneath the curtain to see the man point his gun at her sister's belly. Emilia backed against the stainless-steel counter, shielding the baby with her arms.

What should she do? Cry out? Show herself? Tell that vile, gutless bully that she was the one who could lead him to Nash, not her sister?

The man was screwing a silencer onto the end of his gun. "Don't think I won't do this. According to my sources, she was in the hospital this morning with an injured man. The man I've been paid to find. You choose. Your sister or your baby. Where—?"

Teresa shot to her feet when he aimed the gun again.

But her shout was muffled by the rolling tray table that came flying through the side curtain and smashed into the would-be assassin, knocking him off his feet and crushing him against the storage counter. Nash!

Before the fake cop could get to his feet, Nash's fist

crunched against the man's jaw, driving him back onto the table. But the man kicked out, forcing Nash back. He swung his gun around, but Nash charged his midsection and lifted him off his feet. Teresa ran in to pull Emilia aside as the two men tumbled over the edge of the table and hit the floor. Hard. The gun slid beneath the table. She heard Nash's grunt of pain, cringed at the thud of fist against bone.

She had to help. Nash had had a bullet in him just three days ago. His strength wouldn't last. It wasn't a fair fight.

The men flipped, rolled, knocked over a stool. Emilia dodged their twisting legs while Teresa spotted the medicine dispensary and got an idea. She dashed around the table. "Emilia, what's the combination?"

Her sister rattled off the computer code and Teresa unlocked the cabinet. She grabbed a vial. Peeled open a syringe.

"Teresa!" Emilia warned.

She spun and saw the knife the thug had pulled out.

But Nash was on top again, his fist clamped over the other man's wrist. He banged the hand clutching the knife on the floor—once, twice—until the man released his grip and the weapon skittered away into the next bay.

And then he pressed his forearm against the other man's throat, pinning him to the floor, choking him.

"Who's Graciela's inside man?" he demanded on a wheezing breath. He increased the pressure on the man's throat. "Who told you where to find me?"

The black-haired man with the bloody lip laughed and spit at Nash. *"Son todos los muertos."*

You are all dead.

The moment Nash blinked and swiped the spittle from his face, the other man reared up with a roar. Teresa dropped to her knees and jabbed the loaded syringe into his thigh. The last-ditch rebellion was short-lived. Nash pushed him back to the floor, pinning him until the other man's muscles relaxed and he passed out.

"You don't threaten the pregnant lady, understand?"

Only then did Nash ease his grip and roll off onto the floor beside the unconscious man. With his chest heaving in deep, labored breaths, he pulled the gun from beneath the examination table and sat up.

He braced his elbows against his knees and grinned at her. "Good shootin', Peewee. But I thought I told you to stay put."

"He pointed a gun at my sister and future niece. I wasn't going to lose any of you." Teresa crawled over to him and started to tug at his jacket. "Are you all right? I need to check your stitches."

"Let me do that." Emilia picked up a stack of gauze pads to wipe the mess from Nash's jaw and dab at the bump on his cheek that was oozing blood.

"Sorry, ladies, but there's no time." Nash shrugged off both their efforts and tucked the oversize handgun into his belt. He got up on one knee and rolled the black-haired assailant from one side to the other, checking his pockets. He removed the would-be killer's wallet and opened it. "Angel Sanchez. All the way from Harlingen, Texas. I've heard of the Sanchez brothers. They do a lot of work for Graciela. First time I've met one in person."

Teresa could see there was no badge in his billfold or anywhere else on the unconscious man, either. Her stomach soured as she feared the worst. "Where do you think he got the uniform?"

"Hopefully, he got it from someone's locker. I don't see any bullet holes to indicate he took it off an actual cop. With his DEA badge, our mole could walk right into any KCPD building and help himself." Nash pocketed Sanchez's wallet and cell phone before he unhooked the handcuffs from his belt. "These look real enough."

He flipped Sanchez onto his stomach and pulled his hands behind his back to cuff him. "Peewee, I need you to go find his knife. Dr. Grant, is there anything in here I can gag and restrain this guy with?"

"Yes. And it's Emilia." She opened the storage cabinet and ripped open a packet of IV tubing to hand him. "Will this work?"

"Perfect."

Nash had hog-tied the hit man and righted the stool for Emilia to sit on by the time Teresa had picked up the knife. "Are you all right, Doctor?" he asked, winding a few strips of gauze through the man's mouth to keep him quiet when he regained consciousness.

"Emilia?" Teresa hurried to her sister's side. "You look pale."

"I'm fine." Emilia rubbed the side of her belly. "The baby is still reliving the excitement, however. Oh, this girl can kick." She nodded toward the man on the floor. "Is he the man who's after you?"

"One of them."

She reached for Teresa's hand and squeezed it tight. "So you're not safe yet?"

Nash eyed the sisterly clasp of hands and turned to the door with a blend of regret and alertness stamped on his bruised face. "There's another brother out there somewhere. We need to go. If he's here, there are more on the way. They travel in packs, remember?"

Teresa peered out the door, too, wondering if anyone in the lobby had heard the commotion. "We can't leave her here with him."

Emilia picked up the phone on the counter beside her. "You gave him a full dose of that sedative. He'll be out for a couple of hours. I'm calling security now. I'll be fine. Go."

"It's his friends I'm worried about," Teresa insisted.

Nash agreed. "Don't let security touch that guy." He put Angel Sanchez's wallet on the counter beside the phone. "Call your brother or husband to pick him up. I'm sure he's got a rap sheet a mile long. And there's plenty more they can charge him with today. Ask if they'll keep him in isolation for as long as possible so he can't get word out that he's found me."

Emilia nodded. "I can do that."

"And ask your husband or AJ to stay with you, in case one of Sanchez's buddies shows up to ask you some questions."

"I will."

"Thank you." To Teresa's surprise, Nash leaned down and kissed her sister's cheek. "I owe you and your family more than I can repay."

To her greater surprise, Emilia smiled up at him. "Thank you for protecting my child." Her smile included Teresa. "And my sister."

Nash nodded, dismissing her acceptance and returning to the door to keep watch. Teresa could tell he was antsy to be on their way. But she hated to leave her sister unprotected, despite knowing the man on the floor could no longer harm her. "I'm sorry I brought this danger into your world."

"I told you it wasn't an easy life." Emilia stood to offer one more piece of advice. "I know my sister is trying to prove she's invincible. But she's not. Neither are you, I suspect. Keep each other safe." She wrapped Teresa up in a tight hug. Then she released her and scooted her toward the door. "We have plans for Christmas, remember? You come home to us."

Nash reached for Teresa's hand and linked his fingers with hers. "She will."

Ten minutes later, Teresa drove the silver pickup out of the employee parking garage into the glare of the sun reflecting off the snow outside. With his shaggy beard growth, hat pulled low over his forehead and a pair of sunglasses they'd found in Jake's truck, Nash was practically unrecognizable as the man she'd first pulled out of that ditch. She, too, put on her sunglasses to help mask her face from all the searching eyes who seemed to be at Truman Medical Center today.

It felt weird, wrong, perhaps, to be donning disguises and leaving her family behind to go into hiding with Nash and continue to help in his quest. The fear she'd known when he'd first forced her to do his bidding at gunpoint was gone. But so was any sense of excitement or adventure. That urge to show herself as competent and capable had matured into a sense of duty, a commitment to a cause…or person she believed in.

As she pulled into a line of cars to wait for the traffic light at the parking lot exit to change, her gaze slid across the front seat to Nash. He was busy scrolling through the information on the perp's phone, seeking answers. Her blood warmed in her veins at the sight of his broad shoulders and bowed head. But she chilled again just as quickly.

Emilia was wrong. She wasn't trying to prove her invincibility. Teresa knew she was anything but. She'd fallen in love with Charles Nash. And if anything happened to him, if men like Angel Sanchez got to him before he uncovered the truth, then she could lose him.

And that would be a wound that even her talented sister wouldn't be able to fix.

"You're staring at me, Peewee." His golden-brown eyes tilted up to hers. "I'm not bleeding again, am I?"

"Are you sure Emilia will be safe in the E.R. with that man?" Teresa still felt uneasy about leaving her sister behind to deal with Sanchez's brother and friends.

"She had her husband on the phone before we left," he reminded her. He reached across the center console to squeeze her thigh. "You can call her when we get back to the Seaside Motel to make sure she's okay."

Teresa flashed him a weak smile. "Thanks." She glanced down at the phone in his hand. "Did you find anything?"

"No names. But our Señor Sanchez has a lot of incoming calls from the same number. Three within the past hour."

"Is the number in your black book?" She turned her attention back to traffic as the light changed.

"It's a Houston prefix. I'll check it when we get back to the motel. Maybe Jake's friend Detective Montgomery can run the number for me."

Teresa followed the car in front of her up to the road and turned right just as another car was pulling into the parking lot. What the...? She glanced in her sideview mirror, checked the rearview, too. There was something familiar about the dark-haired man behind the wheel. But he sped away before she could get a second look.

"What is it?"

Probably just her frazzled nerves working overtime, making her see ghosts. "Nothing. Just thinking of what a small world it is."

"Teresa, there are armed men in your hospital looking for us. They threatened your sister and tried to kill me. What did you see?"

Maybe she was smart to be more suspicious of the

people around her. "That car that just passed us. I swear the driver was that drunk who was hitting on me in the Shamrock Bar."

Chapter Twelve

Teresa had forgotten how good a shower could feel, even with bargain-brand soap and shampoo for her hair. She felt revived, refreshed, warm, clean, relatively normal.

Since the Seaside Motel's amenities didn't include a hair dryer, bathrobe or complimentary pajamas, she blotted her wet hair, then twisted it up on top of her head with a towel before dressing in her underwear and jeans. She opened the bathroom door to let the steam out before pulling on a camisole and stepping out to use the mirror to dab some lotion onto her cheeks. She squirted more lotion into her palms, and while she rubbed it into her arms and hands, she let her gaze slide to the mirror to study the man working in the room behind her.

Nash sat in the chair beside the rickety table, jotting notes in his little black book of clues and suspicions. He, too, had showered and was letting the stitching around his wounds air out and dry before he put on a warm shirt to sleep in. This was the first time she'd seen him clean shaven, too. It was a different look from the scruffy bear she was used to seeing. She wouldn't call him handsome, exactly—there were too many hard angles and bruises and bumps. Then there was that slightly crooked mouth that charmed like a little boy when he grinned and molded so perfectly to hers when they kissed.

Maybe not handsome, but masculine, compelling. Sexy.

The shave wasn't the only thing different about him tonight. There was more tan than pale to his skin now that he was feeling better. He seemed to have more energy, more focus.

He'd checked the security of the room and peeked outside several times, ensuring they'd drawn no undue attention from anyone. He'd made a couple of calls to Jake. Nash had given his friend the suspicious number to trace off Angel Sanchez's phone, hoping that would lead back to his contact within the DEA or even get a ping on his brother's location if he was here in Kansas City. He'd given Jake Teresa's description of the driver she'd seen. But a man in a suit with dark brown hair and dark eyes wasn't much to go on. Jake promised to run everything past his friend at KCPD and ask some questions around the bar, as well.

Nash had even trusted her, encouraged her, to make an important phone call of her own to her family. Emilia was home with Justin and their son, Joey, and AJ had Sanchez tied up at Fourth Precinct headquarters for all kinds of questioning related to both the assault at the hospital and the break-in at Teresa's apartment.

Not that AJ was pleased to learn the extent of her involvement with the Graciela cartel or just how much she'd been helping one agent in particular. But he understood undercover work and protecting his family. So he'd sit on Sanchez for now and save lecturing Teresa and strangling Nash for later.

This healthier, warier version of Nash felt different from the man she'd stitched up at her apartment. He was different from the man who'd held on to her last night and wept for the friends he'd lost.

This Nash was prowling, driven, self-sufficient—an intensified version of the man she'd fallen in love with.

And maybe he no longer needed her as much as she needed him.

Suddenly, she was aware of golden-brown eyes meeting hers in the mirror. "I can hear you thinking all the way across the room, Peewee."

Caught staring, caught musing, caught revealing far more of her feelings than a smart woman should, perhaps, Teresa quickly straightened the counter around the sink and headed into the main room. The hour had grown late. They'd eaten the last of the soup and split the last sandwich, and she'd given Nash his pill. "Thanks for cleaning up in here."

He grinned. "You've been cleaning up after me long enough. You okay?"

"I'm just worried about people. Worried about everything. Wishing I could do more." She walked past him to pick up the new Kansas City Chiefs sweatshirt she'd bought for herself at the hospital gift shop.

"I think risking your life to help me and your sister qualifies as more." He closed the black book and tucked it into the go bag on the floor beside him. "There's nothing else we can do until I hear from Jake about tracking down those phone numbers."

"Nothing?"

"Try to get a good night's sleep?" he suggested.

"You need one." Instead of putting on the heavy shirt and removing the damp towel, Teresa gathered up the first-aid supplies and brought them back to set on the table beside Nash. She gently poked at the stitches in his shoulder. They were dry. "I'll get this rebandaged so you can get dressed and go to bed. It'd be ridiculous if you caught a cold now, after everything you've been through."

But when she picked up the first gauze pad, Nash captured her wrist and stopped her. "That's not what I need, Peewee." He pulled her onto his lap. "I'm not cold."

He wasn't. The heat on his skin sizzled beneath the hand she'd braced against his uninjured shoulder. And it wasn't from any trace of fever. Teresa tried to make light of the hyperawareness she suddenly felt expanding every pore of her body. The goose bumps on her arms gave her the perfect excuse. "Well, one of us is cold."

He wound his arms around her, pulling her closer to all that bare skin on his chest. "Is that better?"

Yes, she was warmer. But that dusting of tawny hair across his chest was a prickly caress beneath her sensitive palms, and the sleek ripple of muscle that shifted beneath her hands each time he moved was even more distracting. She tried to remember that she was the nurse and he was the patient, that they'd known each other for only a matter of days, that extraordinarily difficult circumstances in close quarters had probably led to this shared feeling of intimacy. He was the injured man. She was the strong one, right? "What are you doing, Nash?"

He rubbed his hand up and down her arm, chasing away the goose bumps there. "There's something about being locked inside this little room with you that makes me crazy."

"Gee, thanks."

"Your scent is in every corner."

"The smell of soap and antiseptic?"

But as much as she tried to make a joke about the tension that drew them to each other, he wasn't laughing. There wasn't so much as a teasing chuckle in those warm golden eyes as he dipped his head to nuzzle her neck. He inhaled and exhaled softly against the indentation behind her ear, tickling the microscopic hairs there.

"You smell like goodness and home and—" he reached up to release the towel from her hair, sending the long, damp strands tumbling down her back "—all the things I may never get to have in my life."

Teresa turned in his lap. "Don't talk like that. You've gotten another lead with Sanchez's phone. Jake is helping. Justin and AJ are working on the case, too." The glimpse of despair she saw in his eyes touched something much deeper than the physical desire his encompassing warmth and gentle touches were stirring inside her. She brushed her fingertips across the line of his bruised cheekbone and cupped the side of his smooth jaw. "We'll get through this."

He sifted his fingers through her hair, smoothing the long layers over her right shoulder and breast, rolling the curling tips between his thumb and fingertips. "For days, all I've been able to think about is avenging Tommy's and Axel's and Jim's deaths. Exposing a traitor. Protecting all the agents who go up against the cartel. From the moment I drove into that Kansas City warehouse, I've fully expected that I'm going to die trying to get this job done."

"Nash—"

He shushed her with a finger over her lips. His gaze, which had been so fascinated with her hair a moment earlier, landed there. "You have the most beautiful mouth I've ever seen on a woman. When I'm alone in this room with you, and the rest of the world is some distant nightmare outside that door, all I can think about is that kiss we shared yesterday."

Her gaze instinctively zeroed in on his mouth. "You were delirious with fever. You probably aren't remembering it accurately."

At last those firm lips crooked up with a dangerous grin. "How's my temperature now, Nurse Rodriguez?"

"Normal. Your fever broke and hasn't come back since this morning." Was that hushed quiver of anticipation really coming from her throat?

Nash brushed the callused pad of his thumb across her bottom lip, sparking a dozen different nerve endings. His smile grew at her soft gasp. "My eyes are focused? My thoughts are sane? No delusions?"

Her mouth was parched with anticipation. "As far as I can tell, you're...healthy."

"Good. I just wanted to make sure we're clear on this." Then he leaned in, replacing his thumb with his mouth. He stroked his tongue across the curve of her lip. He kissed her gently, then drew the sensitive bow between his lips to suckle and tease. Teresa's breath stuttered in her throat, then rushed out to blend with his. He touched his tongue to hers, retreated, touched her again. With one hand palming her hip and the other buried in the weight of her hair at her nape, he held her in place against his mouth and thighs.

Her fingers dug into the warm skin of his chest. The tips of her breasts pearled into needy nubs at this leisurely seduction of her mouth. The liquid heaviness of growing need settled between her legs. She whimpered in her throat at the thoroughness with which he tasted, aroused, soothed. She squirmed in his lap to find a better angle to meet each kiss, threaded her fingers into his short hair to pull him closer, to increase the pressure, to deepen the kiss.

"Nash?"

"Me, too."

Suddenly, the atmosphere in the room changed. The kiss grew more impatient. Like a match lighting a fuse, Nash's right arm snaked around her waist and he stood. Her bare toes never touched the carpet. He hauled her up to his chest with his good arm and kissed her harder. "Hold on to me, darlin'. Unless you want me to stop."

Teresa willing obeyed, winding her arms around his neck and reconnecting the kiss. His left hand threaded into her hair and his right hand palmed her bottom, holding her body flush against his as he turned, sat on the edge of the bed and fell back with her on top of him.

"Watch your should—" He kissed her into silence. Other than a single grunt when they landed, the man didn't appear to be feeling any pain at all. Her thighs parted around his and he bent his knee slightly, rubbing its solid strength at the juncture there, stoking the pressure and leaving her gasping for release against the salty warmth of his neck.

With his knee trapping her against the flexing heat of his body, he rolled her to the bed beside him. While he kissed her cheeks, her chin, that sensitive bundle of nerves behind her ear, his hands went to work, too. He pushed the knit camisole up to her breasts, stroking his hand along her stomach, exposing her heated skin to the room's cool air. He skimmed the camisole off over her head. And then his hand was on one breast, squeezing, playing. His mouth was on the other, tonguing her to a feverish pitch through the wet satin of her bra.

Teresa bucked beneath the weight of his lower body pinning hers, wanting to be closer, needing to feel more. She laced her fingers through his hair and clutched at his scalp, holding his raspy tongue against the thrusting tip of her breast. There wasn't a cell in her body that wasn't on fire, and all that extra heat seemed to be building in the sensitized weight of her breasts and priming something bigger, hotter, deep inside the heart of her.

As he explored her body with his hands, she tried to take the same liberties with him. She found the stiff bead of a male nipple in the crisp curls on his chest. She discovered the quivering response of her fingertips brushing across the flat of his stomach, dipping beneath the snap of his jeans. She squeezed her legs around the wedge of his thigh and skimmed her palms up his strong arms and back.

When she accidentally brushed her fingers over the wound by his shoulder blade, there was just one little flinch of discomfort. Just one big reminder of what was happening here.

"Nash," she gasped. "We probably shouldn't. You're still on the mend." And though she couldn't quite seem to catch her breath, she braced her hands on the relatively neutral space of his chest and started to shift away. "Just because we—"

"Don't you dare." Nash pulled her right back. He brushed the hair away from her face, looked down into her eyes. "I've never felt as strong as I do when I'm with you. I need you more than I need the truth, more than I need my next breath." He threw one long leg over both of hers, letting her feel the bulge of his arousal at her hip. Very healthy indeed. "Please, Peewee." Although his chest heaved in and out with every deep, ragged breath, brushing against hers, he held himself back. "Will you?"

"Nash, I…" She tiptoed her fingers around his neck, looked up into his handsome, expectant eyes and knew her answer. "I want to call you Charlie. It feels more personal. Is that okay?"

His mouth slowly crooked into a grin. "That's very okay with me."

"And, Charlie?"

"Hmm?"

"No more Peewee, please. Not when we're close like this."

He slipped his hand between them, slowly unzipped her jeans and slid his fingers inside to torment her. "Close like this?"

She clenched her thighs against the pressure of his hand, barely able to speak as the pleasure built inside her. "Yes."

"I've never met anyone like you, Teresa Rodriguez. Strong and gentle, brave and full of fire." He pulled her panties aside, thrust a finger inside her, and she moaned against the fragrant warmth of his chest. "I've never wanted to be with anyone the way I want to be with you."

"Me, either."

"We make a great team, don't we?"

"Yes."

"I've been on assignment or focused on my work for so long that I can't remember the last time I wanted—"

"Charlie?" She pressed a kiss to his chest. Kissed his chin. Pulled his mouth close to hers.

"Yeah?"

"We only have until Christmas, remember? Less talking. More action."

He grinned. "Yes, ma'am."

For several needy, frustrating seconds, they pulled apart to remove the rest of their clothes, to dig a condom from his wallet, to fall back onto the bed together.

And then his mouth closed over hers. Her body melted beneath the beauty of his kiss and the weight of his body moving on top of her and sliding inside. "That's it, darlin'. Let it happen."

There were no more words. Only touches and kisses, moans of need and gasps of pleasure. The heat detonated inside her, and Teresa held on tight, riding the shock waves of pleasure. She held on tighter as Charlie's fingers tangled in her hair, and he groaned with the power of his own release.

Afterward, they drifted off to sleep, still cradled in each other's arms. Her dark hair and the warmth of Charlie's body draped possessively around hers were the only cover she needed.

SOMETIME LATER IN the night, Nash awoke to find a petite package of decadent curves spooned against his chest. When he stroked her long, soft hair down her back, Teresa shivered against him, stirring the interest of his body again.

When he looked down, he found her beautiful dark eyes open, watching him. "Are you okay?" she asked. "You were sleeping pretty hard."

"Always taking care of me, hmm?"

Her fingers drew tantalizing little designs across his chest. "That was the deal, right? I take care of you, and you live long enough to catch the bad guys?" Her gaze shuttered and dropped to the middle of his chest. Her hands stilled. "I think I'm in love with you, Charlie Nash."

His heart swelled at her softly spoken admission, spreading light into his dark world, filling him with a humility and hope he had no business feeling.

Similar words danced across his tongue. But he couldn't bring himself to say them. This woman was too good, too sweet, too important for him to make her any promises he couldn't keep.

Instead he captured her chin between his thumb and finger and tipped her face back up to his. "Teresa…"

Her mouth softened with a beautifully serene smile and she nodded, as if she understood the things he couldn't say. And then she stretched up against his eagerly attentive body and kissed him. This he could do. This he could give her.

Making love the second time was a little more urgent, a little more familiar, a little more poignant. When he buried himself inside her, the lights exploded behind his eyes, and her slick body collapsed on top of his, leaving Nash utterly exhausted. He felt completely happy and strangely bereft.

His life had never been this good, yet it had never been this complicated, either. The rational side of his brain told him that this connection he felt to Teresa was all an illusion, a cosmic lining up of a sexy woman, a dangerous situation, close quarters and a man who might not have many tomorrows.

But the woman in his bed was real. Her bravery and stubbornness and compassion were all real. In his heart, something was telling him that these feelings he had for her were just as real. But he couldn't bring himself to believe that this reality could last. He'd lost too much in his life—his parents, his friends, his faith that there would always be someone who had his back, the security of believing there would be a tomorrow.

But this woman made him believe. For now. For tonight.

If he died tomorrow, he'd die a happy man.

And if he survived this hell and lived to be a hundred, he'd never regret this one perfect night he'd spent with Teresa Rodriguez in his arms.

NASH WAS SNORING contentedly beneath the covers when Teresa stepped out of the bathroom fully dressed. Although her body was a little tired from the extra exercise and fewer hours of sleep she'd gotten last night, she suspected she still had more energy than a man who'd been shot twice less than a week ago.

Besides, she'd heard the empty grumblings in Nash's stomach while he slept. Her own tummy was hungry for breakfast. Making sure the patient ate regularly and kept up his strength was part of a nurse's job, too.

Besides, if she stayed cocooned in bed with Nash much longer, her foolish heart might begin to believe the passion and tenderness they'd shared could last beyond the terms of the partnership they'd made. Nash hadn't made her any promises. And though she had no doubt that the man truly cared for her on some level, she wasn't going to ask for any. There were any number of reasons why a relationship between them wouldn't work—the simplest being that they lived in two different cities, the most difficult being that a drug cartel wanted him dead.

So for now, she'd tuck her heart away and take care of the practicalities that had been her responsibility from the moment they'd met.

After bundling up in her coat and pulling her billfold from her bag, she crossed over to the bed and smiled down at the familiar tawny stubble shading Nash's jaw. She caught her ponytail behind her neck and leaned down to press a kiss to the crooked line of his mouth.

One golden eye popped open, then the other. He smiled. "Morning, darlin'."

"Good morning, Charlie."

The smile vanished and he sighed in disappointment. "You have all your clothes on."

Teresa laughed and dodged away when he reached for her. "I'm hungry and we're out of food. I'm going down to the office to see if there's anything breakfastlike in the vending machines there."

The sheet and blanket pooled around his hips as he

sat up. He gently stretched some of the stiffness from his left shoulder and nodded toward the window. Nakedness aside, he sternly reminded her of the safety precautions that had become ingrained in her during these past few days together. "Make sure you check the parking lot before you go out. Account for all the cars we saw last night. If there are any extras, you'll have to wait a few minutes for me to go with you."

Determined to allow him the rest he needed, Teresa pulled aside the dusty drape and peeked out. "The two work trucks are gone, and it looks like Mr. Moscatelli is back. Otherwise, they're the same."

Nash nodded his approval, but he wasn't ready to quit the protection job. He reached for his jeans and shorts at the foot of the bed. "All right. Straight there and straight back. If you're gone too long—"

"You'll come looking for me. I'll be back in a couple of minutes. Long enough for you to get dressed."

Teresa opened the door and stepped onto the sidewalk, quickly closing the door behind her. The air felt particularly brisk and damp this morning. Shivering almost at once, she pulled up her hood and stuffed her hands into her pockets. It was probably the shock of the cold after spending such a toasty night in bed that made the wintry morning feel particularly harsh. Another reason not to tarry any longer on her errand than necessary.

She hurried her steps in front of building A, checking windows the way she'd seen Nash do. But there was no movement to any of the curtains. No curious eyes on her. The traffic on the street looked like any other morning in the city. Drivers were focused on getting to work, not slowing down for a look at the Seaside's cheesy decor.

A blast of heat and the noisy chatter of the morning news on TV welcomed her into the motel office. Although there was no one sitting behind the counter at the desk, the television and flask were certain signs that Mr. Moscatelli had paid whatever fine or bail was asked of him, and the police had allowed him to return to work at the family business. The door to the laundry-and-storage room behind the counter stood slightly ajar. Maybe he was taking a break from his television shows and doing a load of laundry.

Breathing easier at the lack of company, Teresa pulled out her billfold and inspected the two vending machines set up in the nook beside the ice machine. Her choices were limited and the prices were steep, but she inserted her cash and got a couple of granola bars and bottles of orange juice for a relatively nutritious, if not necessarily filling, meal.

She was stuffing the bottles of OJ into her pockets when she heard the gravelly voice behind her. "That's her. She's the one in 6A."

She turned to see Mr. Moscatelli stepping out of the laundry room. A younger man, dressed in a suit and a long winter coat, slipped some cash into the old man's hand as he stepped out around him. Wariness turned to surprise, then confusion, then to guarded fear.

The man in the car yesterday, the obnoxious drunk from the Shamrock Bar, perfectly sober now, walked to the end of the counter.

Teresa eyed the distance to the door as the man approached. "You. Are you following me? Who are you?"

He paused at the counter to stuff his hands into his pockets. He pulled one back out but left the other in his slacks. His charming smile and delay in answering were altogether creepy. He flipped open a wallet she recognized, dark brown and narrow, like the one Nash carried. Like the ones Cruz Moreno and Jesse Puente had both shown her.

Oh, no.

His wallet held a badge he clipped onto the chest pocket of his coat. *The mole.* "Good morning, Mrs. Smith. Or should I say Miss Rodriguez? You've led me and my friends on quite the merry chase. But I believe you are the key to getting what I want."

What was in the other hand, a gun? She drifted toward the door. "How do you know my name?"

"Police reports. An introduction at the Shamrock. A chat with one of my associates at the hospital."

How long had she been gone? One minute? Two? Five? How long before Nash got worried and came storming in here to find her? How long before he walked straight into a trap? She had to warn him.

"I forget my manners. Allow me to introduce myself." He tapped his badge and took a step forward. "I work for the Drug Enforcement Administration out of Houston, Texas. I'm Agent Tommy Delvecchio."

Nash's dead friend?

The young man he'd wept for?

He was the traitor?

"You're dead."

Agent Delvecchio grinned. "A bladder of blood and enough crossfire to keep Nash from checking my vital signs? Not so much. Of course, this whole week would have been much easier if the men who hired me had just done their job and killed him in the first place."

It would destroy Nash to learn who had betrayed him and his men. One of his own team. Part of his family.

But she wouldn't let him die.

She was inches from the door now. Closer to escape than to the man advancing on her.

And then she heard the squealing of tires on the pavement and glanced out to see a black SUV jumping the curb and speeding into the motel parking lot.

Tommy Delvecchio pulled his left hand from his pocket, showing her the cell phone he'd used to send one of his cartel buddies a text.

"Six-A," Tommy deadpanned.

Teresa hurled the two bottles at his head, forcing him to duck. She shoved open the door as a second SUV veered around the corner into the driveway. She ran across the slick asphalt, praying, hoping.

"Nash! Nash!"

THE HAIRS ON the back of Nash's neck stood on end. Teresa had been gone too long. He fastened the buckle on his belt, securing the Smith & Wesson at his side, and reached for his shirt. If she wasn't back here before he got his coat on, then he was marching down to the office, throwing her over his shoulder and hauling her back to the secure confines—

The sound of speeding tires screaming for traction on the snowy asphalt turned his blood to ice.

He was already running to his bag for backup when he heard Teresa shouting his name. "Nash! Nash!"

He whipped aside the drapes and swore. Teresa was charging across the parking lot. A black SUV was barreling toward the building from the other direction.

Nash jammed the shells into his shotgun and threw open the door. He braced the butt of the gun against his good shoulder and took aim. "Get down!"

Boom! The recoil jolted through him, but he'd hit the front tire.

"Nash!"

He saw a blur of turquoise coat in his side vision as he

aimed at the fishtailing car and pulled the second trigger. "Stay back!"

With the vehicle disabled, the driver shot to hell and the passenger clinging to whatever he could grab, the big SUV flipped, crashing into the fence around the pool and knocking over a palm tree. Nash dropped the shotgun and drew his sidearm, cradling the pistol between his hands and advancing out the door as a second SUV braked to a stop in front of the office.

"Teresa?"

"Charlie?"

Her strangled gulp squeezed his heart in an iron fist. He turned and saw the impossible.

His aim went instinctively toward the movement at the corner of the building. A man's arm, cinched around Teresa's neck. A gun pointed to her head.

For a split second, his brain refused to work. He lowered his gun from the shield Teresa created, raised it again to the man who held her captive. "Tommy?"

The eager young agent who'd been so pleased with his idea for helping a field veteran like him was still looking pretty pleased with himself. But he didn't look young or naive as he pushed the barrel of his Glock against Teresa's temple and backed up with his prisoner to the second SUV. "You and I will talk later, Nash."

Nash followed them a step, glanced down at the trusting hope in Teresa's dark eyes and stopped. An unaccustomed fear sucker punched him, and anger raised bile in his throat. "Let her go."

"Somehow I don't think you'll come quietly if I do." The driver of the SUV pushed the door open behind Tommy. Teresa tugged at his arm around her neck, but neither it nor the gun was budging. "You're the one Berto wants. You've been so much trouble that he's here in town to finish the job himself."

Nash didn't know if he was that good a shot with one bum arm to trust that he could take out that rat bastard without hitting Teresa. "If you hurt her—"

The wail of sirens sounded in the distance. Someone must have called in the speeding cars and gunfire.

Tommy had reached the car with Teresa. Nash's gaze darted down to Teresa. *I love you, Peewee.* "I will protect you," he vowed.

"That's what I'm counting on." Tommy laughed and shoved her inside, climbing in behind her. "Gotta go."

"I'm comin' for you, Tommy." The car door slammed shut, and Nash charged. But the driver floored it, racing forward. Nash dove into a snowdrift to avoid getting hit. The big SUV churned up slush and ice as it made a big U-turn around the pool. Nash got to his feet and chased after it, getting off a couple of low shots at its rear tires before it reached the street and careened into traffic.

"Son of a… Teresa!" He reversed course and ran back to the truck.

The keys! Hell, Teresa had them. He banged on the glass with the butt of his gun. He could hot-wire the thing if he could get inside. He struck it again, desperate to get to her.

The sirens were on top of him now. Red-and-blue lights flashed off the glass.

"Police! Drop your weapon!"

He smashed the glass and the window shattered.

"Drop it!"

Nash raised his hands. "I'm a federal agent. A woman's been kidnapped."

But the blue suit wasn't listening. All he saw was the

gun in Nash's hand. The shotgun on the ground. The wrecked car with the bloodied driver and passenger.

"On your knees," the older cop ordered.

What was he supposed to do? Shoot two real cops?

With a nod that he was complying, Nash went down to his knees on the cold asphalt and set the gun on the ground beside him.

"These two are dead, Paulie." The younger cop moved away from the wrecked SUV.

Nash glanced over at the car, recognizing the faces. Maybe a little intel would convince them to let him go. "The vics are Santiago Vargas and Davey Gallion. They're a cartel lieutenant and enforcer. Look 'em up. They both have warrants."

"Yeah, and who are you? The tooth fairy?"

"I'm a federal agent. I've worked undercover on a task force to nail these guys. My badge is in the room." The black cop picked up the shotgun and went inside while the older one tucked away Nash's sidearm and pulled his arms behind his back to handcuff him. Although it hurt like hell to bend his arm that way, it hurt worse knowing Teresa had been taken hostage. "An accomplice of theirs just kidnapped an innocent woman. You have to let me go."

The younger cop returned with his go bag. "Hell, Paulie. He's got a whole arsenal of firearms in here."

The cop named Paulie dragged Nash to his feet. "You sure you're not some kind of enforcer, too?"

He pushed Nash toward the squad car. "Look inside the bag. My badge is in there. I'm a federal agent."

"Okay, tooth fairy. We'll look."

They put him in the back of the squad car until the younger cop had cleared the motel room and Paulie had called dispatch for the M.E. and backup. By then Teresa, and any chance of catching Tommy before he took her to Graciela, was gone.

Chapter Thirteen

"Sorry about the makeshift accommodations, Agent Nash." The young police officer, DeShawn Britt, knocked on the door of the third-floor interview room to bring him a cup of coffee and apologize. "We had a tornado blow through here this past summer. It took out a good chunk of the building and we're still repairing—"

"I know." The tight quarters and the one-way mirror didn't bother Nash, other than it didn't leave him much room to pace. There wasn't an officer he'd met yet in KCPD's Fourth Precinct offices who hadn't told him some chapter about the storm that had hit downtown Kansas City. He didn't wish that kind of hardship on anyone. But right now he didn't care if a blizzard hit the city. It wasn't going to stop him from doing what he needed to do. "I've already been waiting half an hour and time is critical. It's imperative that I talk to—"

The interview room door opened, and a short muscular detective with black hair and a fitted black fatigue sweater stepped in. Nash had seen him only once before, a brief glimpse of his profile in Teresa's apartment. But the man was on duty now. And judging by the unrevealing expression on his face and the hardware he wore holstered beneath each arm, Detective AJ Rodriguez was serious business.

"I hear you're looking for me." Nash could believe that more than one suspect had quaked in his boots in this room as the veteran detective walked in, followed by a big bruiser of a blond cop. AJ dismissed the uniformed officer and nodded toward the other man. "My partner, Josh Taylor."

"Good to meet you, Nash." Josh stepped forward to shake his hand while AJ moved to the opposite side of the interview table and crossed his arms over the badge that hung around his neck. Josh noticed the sizing up, too, and laughed. "Good luck."

Nash might have stood a head taller than Teresa's brother, but he had to respect that the guy could take him. Especially if he had blondie here to back him up.

Nah. AJ Rodriguez looked tough enough to take him all on his own. Nash pulled up to his full height, ready to stand his ground.

"You kidnapped my sister?" AJ accused.

"I needed a nurse. She saved my life."

"And now you got her kidnapped by a drug cartel?"

"Once she made contact with my office and alerted the mole to where I was hiding, I knew they'd use her to get to me. She was safer with me than out there on her own, unprotected."

"They're using her, all right." AJ fisted his hands on top of the table and leaned forward. "Is this how the DEA runs their undercover ops?"

Nash hadn't expected this conversation to go smoothly. But he didn't have time to soothe egos or earn Brownie points with Teresa's family. "I'm not going to try to explain how I'm worthy of your sister. I'm not. And I'm not going to explain how desperate and dangerous life gets when an undercover op blows up in your face. If you're the vet Teresa claims, you already know that." Nash mirrored AJ's position at the table. "I need your help."

AJ and Detective Taylor listened while Nash gave them a sit rep on Tommy Delvecchio, the Gracielas and the price on his head.

"Puente will have the DEA there. But he's more interested in rounding up Graciela's men and getting me out of there." Nash looked big brother straight in the eye, sending a message between men, not cops. "You and I have the same goal."

AJ nodded. "To save Teresa."

"I have a plan. Will you help?"

"Josh, you working tonight?"

The blond cop grinned. "I'm always on the job when you are, buddy. I've got time for a little backup."

Nash nodded his appreciation. Neither man had to like him or trust him, but he was counting on them to care about Teresa. "I promised her she'd be home safe to her family by Christmas. That's one promise I intend to keep. I'll do whatever it takes to make that happen."

Josh excused himself from the room and got on the phone to call for some of the support they'd need. Talking cop to cop now, Nash pulled his black book from his pocket and tossed it onto the table.

AJ picked it up and thumbed through the pages of notes while Nash explained. "I want you to give that to my boss, Jesse Puente. His number's in the front. It spells out who the mole is in our office. If I can't take Tommy Delvecchio out when I go to that warehouse, I need you to give that to him."

"All right." AJ stuffed the book into the back pocket of his jeans. "Let's do it."

Nash pulled out his phone and punched in the number that had been repeated so often on Angel Sanchez's phone. The same number had been found in Santiago Vargas's phone, as well. He placed it on speaker mode and set the phone on the table.

As expected, Tommy Delvecchio picked up. "Nash. Problem with the cops? For a while there, I didn't think they were going to let you make your phone call to me. Your little girlfriend has been a bit of a handful."

That sounded like his girl. *Give 'em trouble, darlin'.* "Put her on. I need to know she's okay."

"Of course." There was a scuffle of movement, and then a soft, familiar voice.

"Charlie?"

"I'm coming to get you, Peewee."

Instead of crying or begging for help or even saying *I love you* again, she shouted into the phone as it was being taken away. "I counted eight men, including your friend. Two outside and—"

Bless her brave heart.

Nash couldn't be prouder. Or more afraid. He was going to kill Tommy if one hair on her beautiful head had been hurt.

Tommy was back on the phone. "Señor Graciela is anxious to see you. While he's pleased you took care of Señor Vargas for him, you're still a blot on the family pride." He gave Nash the address of a warehouse and AJ nodded, indicating he knew its location. "Shall I assume you're on your way?"

"Yeah. I'm ready to make the trade."

Nash disconnected the call and put away the phone.

But AJ stopped him before he could reach the door. "Are you in love with my sister?"

"Yes."

He thought AJ would need some time to process that admission. Nash was damn sure he wasn't the man AJ would choose for his baby sister. He even thought, as the overprotective big brother, he might want to take a swing at Nash. AJ would make a hell of a poker player because right now he wasn't giving away a thing.

The detective simply nodded at Nash and opened the door. "Let's go get her."

"WELCOME, NASH." TOMMY DELVECCHIO was grinning like the Cheshire cat as he locked a pair of handcuffs around Nash's wrists. Nash clenched his fists together in front of him, testing the strength of the steel restraints while Julian Sanchez patted him down and took both his Smith & Wesson and the gun strapped to his ankle and set them on the rusted tire rack beside the door.

Nash could see his breath in the cold air of the run-down warehouse near the Missouri River that looked a lot like that chop shop where he'd been wounded. Tommy must have scouted out both locations when he'd set up that ambush and faked his death. Tommy might have been a lying scumbag cheat, but in a lot of ways, he was predictable.

Maybe Nash could use that predictability to his advantage. "Nice digs, Tommy. So this is what your dealings with the Gracielas have bought you?"

"Actually, it's bought me a nice place down on Isla Tenebrosa. No extradition to the U.S. from there. And now that I'm officially dead, I'm going to start a new life and enjoy the payoff." Tommy shrugged. "This is just a business meeting, fulfilling the last of my obligation to Señor Graciela."

"No wires, but he's wearing a vest," Julian reported. "Do you want me to take it off him?"

Tommy picked up the two guns, sliding one into each coat pocket. "No. Let him enjoy the illusion of having a chance at surviving. A bullet to the head will kill him as surely as one to the heart."

"Where is she?" Nash wanted eyes on Teresa, to see for himself that she hadn't been harmed and to try to somehow communicate his crazy idea for a plan where they could both get out of here alive.

"Now, now. You've forced me to be very patient. You can do the same. There's a certain procedure that needs to be followed." Tommy nodded to Julian to shove Nash into step ahead of him before following them into the warehouse's main storage area.

It was a cavernous room with a second-story loft running along the east and west walls. He saw two more armed guards up there, one on each side, watching out the windows. There wasn't much cover in the abandoned space, just a few stacks of pallets and empty crates and one rust bucket of a forklift off to one side.

But the old desk in the middle of the concrete floor was the most important spot in the room.

"Nash?" Teresa stood up from the chair beside the desk.

"Sit down." Berto Graciela sat in the chair behind the desk. As soon as he pointed to the man Nash assumed was his bodyguard du jour, the hired gun pushed Teresa back in her seat.

She instantly shrugged her shoulder away from the goon's big hand. Her wrists were tied in front of her, the hood of her turquoise coat billowed around her shoulders, and several strands of hair had worked loose from her ponytail and fell around her face. Nash met her gaze with the shadow of a grin. Good. He wasn't surprised to see she'd put up a bit of a fight, but he was glad it hadn't been enough to get herself hurt.

"We need to stop meeting like this, Peewee." Nash

raised his fists in front of him and jerked at the handcuffs. Her dark eyes widened, sensing he was trying to communicate a message. *That's it, darlin'. Figure it out. Play along with me. I'll keep you safe.*

"Here, Nash." Tommy walked past him to the desk, setting the two guns and the keys to the handcuffs on the corner of the desk. Teresa's gaze drifted over to the bounty Tommy had taken from him.

But Nash's gaze had settled on a more imminent threat. Tommy drew back his coat and pulled a knife from his belt. "Tommy!"

Nash lurched forward. Julian Sanchez caught him by his bum arm and jerked him back into place. The pain that blossomed in his shoulder was nothing compared to the fear of seeing Tommy open that knife and lean over Teresa. But Tommy lifted Teresa's hands from the desktop and sliced through the rope that bound her. He straightened and tossed the bindings at Nash's feet. "A gesture of trust."

"You think I'm ever going to trust you again?"

Tommy took Teresa by the arm and pulled her up beside him. "This is the deal we made. Her life for yours."

"Nash, no," Teresa wailed. She dropped her face into her hands. Was she coughing? Or crying?

Wait. Teresa Rodriguez crying? What was going on here? The woman Nash knew was more likely to elbow Tommy in the gut than break down in tears.

But whatever game she was playing, Nash was the only one who seemed to realize her behavior was off. Was this some kind of reply to his silent message about her brother and a boatload of reinforcements from KCPD and the DEA taking out the two guards outside and lying in wait for his signal to storm the building and rescue her?

"This is all very touching." Tommy jerked Teresa's

hands away from her face and pulled her to one side. "I'm glad you made a friend here in Kansas City. But Señor Graciela would like to say a few words to you before we complete the transaction."

Berto Graciela rose from his chair behind the desk. The scalp beneath his thinning gray hair was pink from the cold. But there was nothing vulnerable about his dark eyes and grim expression. He straightened the scarf at his neck and strolled around the table to face Nash. "You made me lose face in my own organization. You and your men were undermining me at every turn."

Nash glared down at the shorter man. "Just doing our job."

Graciela nodded at Julian Sanchez, and the enforcer delivered a kick to the back of Nash's legs, driving him down to his knees. He grunted as the concrete jarred through his body. Teresa's soft gasp of concern was real this time. Nash lifted his gaze to hers and warned her to stay put. It wasn't as if he hadn't survived worse punishment.

Now that Berto held the superior position, he held out his hand toward his bodyguard. The man pulled a gun from his belt and placed it in his boss's hand. Berto slipped a bullet into the firing chamber and pointed the gun at Nash's head. "I had to put a stop to it."

Nash refused to flinch. AJ was waiting for his signal, but he needed to know the truth first. For Torres and Richter. For Teresa. For her sister Emilia and all the lives Tommy's treachery had endangered. "So you recruited Tommy Delvecchio. He told you who our agents were so you could kill them. Then he staged his own death so the DEA would never know he was the traitor."

Berto nodded. "I lost millions of dollars because of you. The people who worked for me lost faith in my leadership. I want to end your miserable life right now, but your death will serve me better if I take you home and kill you in front of my men. Then everyone will know that I am the rightful chief of the Graciela organization."

Nash looked away from the barrel of Berto's gun and glared at Tommy. "We were your family."

Tommy shrugged. "Yes, well, Señor Graciela paid me an obscene amount of money to become a part of his."

"Captain Puente had no idea you were a traitor."

"No one did." Tommy seemed to enjoy confessing his sins almost as much as Nash needed to hear them. "But I couldn't finish the job I was hired to do, because you wouldn't die."

Nash spared a loving glance for Teresa before lifting his gaze to Berto Graciela. "All right. Let's do this. I know you're a man of your word, even if Agent Delvecchio isn't. You put a hit out on me, not her. Let her go and I'll come with you without a fight."

Berto nodded to his bodyguard, and the man went to get Teresa. But Tommy, the weaselly scumbag, wouldn't let go. "She's just the bait. You can't really let her go. She's seen our faces and knows our names. Her brother's a cop."

The older man turned, clearly disgusted with having his word challenged. "If she is a problem for you, Mr. Delvecchio, you take care of it. She is of no concern to me."

"Fine. We'll let her go." He checked his watch. "Your plane is ready at the airport. We need to get going anyway."

Interesting. So Tommy was willing to be responsible for several good men's deaths as long as he didn't have to pull the trigger himself. Nash could work that kind of cowardice into his plan.

Tommy shoved Teresa into the bodyguard's chest, and the man started dragging her toward the front exit. But Teresa had never been one to simply go quietly along. "Wait. I want to say goodbye to him first."

The bodyguard looked to Berto. Berto nodded. He lowered his gun as the bodyguard released Teresa and she ran to him. "Somehow it makes me feel better to know that someone will mourn your passing, Señor Nash. Just remember, you are the cause of her suffering."

Nash swore he heard Teresa mutter, "Oh, shut up." She helped him to his feet and tucked herself inside the loop of his bound arms. Her hands reached up to cup either side of his jaw and angle his face down to hers. "I love you, Charlie Nash. If you get out of this alive, you come back to me. You owe me."

He looked down at her with all the love he possessed. "I know, darlin'. I'm good for it. I promise. You are the bravest woman I know."

He met her halfway when she pulled his face down to hers to share one last beautiful kiss. She thrust her tongue into his mouth. And something more. That sneaky little witch. It wasn't necessary, but she'd just made his job a lot easier.

Nash's teeth clamped down on the hard metal of the key she'd swiped from the corner of the desk.

He pushed the key into the pocket of his cheek and pulled away. "I love you, Teresa."

Then the bodyguard was pulling her away. Tommy followed them toward the door. Berto nodded to Julian to stand back. As soon as Sanchez released him, Berto lowered the gun and pulled the trigger.

"Nash!" Teresa cried, breaking away from her captor.

The bullet ripped straight through Nash's thigh, collapsing him to the floor. "Now I feel better, and he will be less trouble to us." He handed the gun off to Julian Sanchez. "Bring him."

But that first gunshot was the signal AJ had been waiting for.

A battering ram broke open the front door. "KCPD!" A window shattered overhead. "Drop your weapons! On the ground! Now!"

"Nash!" The moment Teresa reached him, Nash threw his arms around her, dragging her beneath him, shielding her with his vest and body as a dozen of her brother's closest friends stormed the building.

Julian Sanchez and the bodyguard returned fire and were instantly put down. Berto raised his hands over his head and dropped to his knees. Tommy dove behind the desk as several more shots were fired.

"Clear!" The two guards up top had been subdued.

Uniformed officers and detectives swarmed in. Captain Puente and Cruz Moreno went straight to Berto Graciela and put him in handcuffs. While Cruz read Graciela his rights and escorted him out the door, the captain hurried over to Nash and helped him sit up. "You're a hard man to find." He winked at the petite woman clutched to Nash's side. "Good to see you again, Ms. Rodriguez. I trust we can be straightforward with each other now?"

She was scrambling to free herself, but Nash wouldn't allow it. "Yes, sir. Sorry I couldn't tell you everything."

"You were protecting your partner. Protecting the mission."

Nash turned and pressed a kiss to Teresa's temple, thanking her, beaming with pride at Captain Puente's praise.

The captain glanced down at the blood staining Nash's jeans. "How many pieces is this guy in?"

Teresa shook her head. "Too many."

Josh Taylor, the big cop Nash had met only that morning, stood up from behind the desk. "I think this is one of yours, Nash."

Teresa and Captain Puente helped Nash to his feet at the sound of Tommy's wailing. With their help, he limped over to Detective Taylor to find Tommy handcuffed and rolling on the floor, holding his side, bleeding. His frightened expression made him look a lot like the kid Nash had felt so much grief and guilt over only twenty-four hours earlier. "I'm shot," Tommy whined. "I'm shot."

Josh shrugged his big shoulders. "As far as I can tell, it's just a graze across his rib cage."

Holding Teresa beneath his arm, her strength supporting his, Nash shook his head. He had no pity for the traitor he'd finally exposed. He simply looked down on the man who'd sold out Nash and his team and grinned. "I knew you weren't ready to be a field agent. You're not even smart enough to wear your vest."

Puente wasn't in a joking mood as he hauled Tommy to his feet. "You and I are going to do some major debriefing, Mr. Delvecchio. I don't envy your situation. There's not a cop in Texas who's going to be on your side. And I doubt the cartel is going to be thrilled that you didn't finish the job they paid you to do."

"Captain." Tommy was pleading with him as he and Detective Taylor carted him away. "You've got to give me some kind of protection. I can give you intel on the Gracielas. I've got names on at least…"

Just when Nash thought it might all finally be over, AJ Rodriguez sauntered up on noiseless footsteps, holstering one of his guns beneath his left arm. When he reached for Teresa, Nash didn't try to hold on to her.

"Good work, little one." AJ wrapped her up in a tight hug and kissed her cheek. Big brother was almost smiling when he pulled away. "Look at my baby sister bringin' down a drug lord. You said eight men. We've got them all accounted for, all in custody. Ambulances are on the way."

Nash leaned his hip on the edge of the desk, taking the pressure off his throbbing leg. "You boys know how to put on a good show here in K.C. I appreciate the backup."

"I did it for my sister, cowboy. Not you. But I'm grateful you made sure she didn't get hurt." With a grudging respect and a whole lot of gratitude that was completely mutual, AJ reached out to shake Nash's hand. Then he lowered his gaze to the blood oozing down the side of Nash's jeans. "Is your boyfriend okay?"

"My boy—?" Teresa beamed a big smile. She threw her arms around her brother. "Thank you, AJ. I love you."

"I hope you know what you're in for, Nash," AJ warned, smiling at Teresa as Josh Taylor called him away.

Looked as though he might pass muster with Teresa's family after all.

He reached for Teresa as soon as they were alone. But she knelt down in front of him instead, ripping open the bullet hole in his pant leg to inspect his wound. "Looks like a through-and-through. It's not bleeding enough to indicate the bullet nicked an artery. But you still need—"

"To go to the hospital. I know." Enough. Enough distance, enough interruptions, enough waiting to know for certain that she was finally safe. Nash pulled her to her feet and hauled her right up to his chest, claiming that beautiful mouth in a kiss.

Endless moments later, she pulled away, smiling. "Seriously, Nash? You need to stop getting shot. You should just ask me out on a date."

Epilogue

December 25

DEA agent Charles Nash stepped off the third-floor elevator at Kansas City's Truman Medical Center and strode down the hallway. Well, he moved with as much purpose as a man with healing bullet wounds to his shoulder and both legs could.

He'd been back in Houston for a few days, writing up reports, attending his friends' funerals, making some big decisions. He'd even done a little Christmas shopping.

He was a Texas boy, born and raised, but his heart was here in Missouri. So he'd booked an early-morning flight to KCI. Now he was here with a bag of gifts in his hand and a transfer request to the Kansas City office of the DEA in his pocket.

He didn't have to be a cop to figure out where the party was. He followed the sounds of Christmas music and laughter to the common room of the children's ward. He unbuttoned his heavy coat, pulled off his new black Stetson and inhaled a steadying breath before stepping into the brightly lit room.

He saw Teresa first, dressed in light green hospital scrubs with a red-and-green holiday scrub jacket. She sat at a table near the Christmas tree with Laila Alvarez and two other young patients, playing some kind of board game that involved lots of laughter.

When Teresa saw him in the doorway and stood, the din in the room suddenly quieted. That awkward moment of being the uninvited guest showing up at the party sent a shiver of nerves down Nash's spine.

But the moment passed the instant Teresa smiled at him.

Suddenly, he wasn't the outsider who'd brought danger and death to their city. He was a friend. He was welcome.

Emilia Rodriguez-Grant toddled over to give him a hug. "Merry Christmas, Nash. There's plenty of food and punch. Make yourself at home."

He met her husband, Justin Grant, and their son, Joey. He met other sisters and husbands and nieces and nephews. Josh Taylor and his wife and two daughters welcomed him. And then AJ Rodriguez walked up to him with his wife and sons.

AJ shook his hand. "Merry Christmas, Nash."

"Merry Christmas, AJ."

And while he appreciated the offers to take his coat and bring him cookies, Nash was here for just one reason. Well, two.

He'd never played Santa Claus before, but he had a bag of gifts he was eager to deliver. He crossed the room to the game table and knelt down beside Laila Alvarez's wheelchair. He pulled the big box from the top of his bag and set it on her lap. "I told you I owed you one for hiding me in your room that day. I'm a man who repays his debts and keeps his promises." Her soft brown eyes were wide with anticipation. "Open it."

The little girl made quick work of the bow and tissue paper inside. "Mom! Dad! It's a cowboy hat." Nash took the smaller version of the hat he'd worn and placed it over the girl's knit cap. She pushed herself up out of her wheelchair and fell against Nash, wrapping her frail arms around his neck. "Thank you, Mr. Nash."

"You're welcome, darlin'." He carefully set her back in her chair and stood, turning to Teresa. He tried not to let the sheen of tears shining in her eyes get to him. "I brought some other gifts. To replace the ones that got damaged in your apartment. I didn't know what you had. There's some stuff for boys and girls both in here."

When the children in the room hurried to the tree to open the new gifts, Teresa finally moved around the table. She slid her arms beneath his coat and wound them around his waist, leaning against his chest. "You didn't have to do that."

"Yeah, I did." Nash pressed a kiss to the crown of her hair and hugged her right back. "Merry Christmas."

"Merry Christmas, Charlie."

He had one more gift from the jewelry store tucked away in his pocket for Teresa. But he'd wait until later, when they were alone, before he'd ask if she'd accept it.

Right now there were too many children and family members and friends around, all enjoying the celebration.

"These are the best presents ever." Proudly wearing her new hat, Laila spun her chair around. "Did you get what you wanted for Christmas, Teresa?"

Teresa leaned back against Nash's arms, tilted her face up to his and smiled. "I did."

* * * * *

Don't miss USA TODAY *bestselling author Julie Miller's upcoming miniseries,*
THE PRECINCT: COLD CASE,
coming in 2015!

#1533 DELIVERANCE AT CARDWELL RANCH
Cardwell Cousins • by B.J. Daniels

When Deputy Sheriff Austin Cardwell rescues a woman with no memory in a blizzard, it's only the beginning. Austin vows to uncover her true identity...before her violent past destroys any hope of a future together.

#1534 KIDNAPPING IN KENDALL COUNTY
Sweetwater Ranch • by Delores Fossen

After her investigation into her daughter's kidnapping blows FBI Agent Austin Duran's cover, rancher's daughter Rosalie McKinnon must team up with the rogue cowboy—the very man who once cost Rosalie everything.

#1535 COLD CASE IN CHEROKEE CROSSING
by Rita Herron

Desperate to save her brother from death row, Avery Tierney turns to Texas Ranger Jaxon Ward for help to clear him—but investigating Avery's tragic past will put both their lives and hearts in danger....

#1536 CHRISTMAS JUSTICE
by Robin Perini

Can on-the-run CIA analyst Laurel McCallister and mysterious Sheriff Garrett Galloway uncover the identity of a traitor before the past catches up with them?

#1537 WITNESS PROTECTION
The Campbells of Creek Bend • by Barb Han

First rule of Witness Protection—*never* get involved with the person under protection. But when U.S. Marshal Nick Campbell grows too close to witness Sadie Brooks, how far will he go to save the woman he can't stop thinking about?

#1538 EAGLE'S LAST STAND
Copper Canyon • by Aimée Thurlo

Scarred by life, and from a recent deadly assault, undercover FBI agent Rick Cloud returns home only to find his father murdered and his family under attack. Catching the killer might just cost him Kim Nelson, the one woman who can heal his damaged heart....

"Maybe you don't understand the fine line between snooping and jail. Breaking and entering is—"

"I'm going with you." Donning a hat and gloves, Gillian turned to look at him.

Austin was smiling at her as if amused.

"What?" she said, suddenly feeling uncomfortable under his scrutiny. She knew it was silly. He'd seen her at her absolute worst.

"You just look so...cute," he said. "Clearly, breaking the law excites you."

She smiled in spite of herself. It had been a while since a man had complimented her. But it wasn't breaking the law that excited her.

She breathed in the freezing air. It stung her lungs, but made her feel more alive than she had in years. Fear drove her steps along with hope.

At the dark alley, Austin slowed. It was late enough that there were lights on in the houses.

"Come on," Austin said, and they started to turn down the alley.

A vehicle came around the corner, moving slowly. Gillian felt the headlights wash over them, and she let out a worried sound as she froze in midstep.

Her moment of panic didn't subside when she saw that it was a sheriff's department vehicle.

"Austin?" she whispered, not sure what to do.

He turned to her and pulled her into his arms. Her mouth opened in surprise, and the next thing she knew, he was kissing her. At first, she was too stunned to react. But after a moment, she put her arms around his neck and lost herself in the kiss.

As the headlights of the sheriff's car washed over them, she let out a small helpless moan as Austin deepened the kiss, drawing her even closer.

The sheriff's car went on past, and she felt a pang of regret. Slowly, Austin drew back a little. His gaze locked with hers, and for a moment they stood like that, their quickened warm breaths coming out in white clouds.

"Sorry."

She shook her head. She wasn't sorry. She felt…lightheaded, happy, as if helium-filled. She thought she might drift off into the night if he let go of her.

"Are you okay?" he asked, looking worried.

She touched the tip of her tongue to her lower lip. "Great. Never better."

Find out what happens next in
DELIVERANCE AT CARDWELL RANCH
by New York Times *bestselling author B.J. Daniels,*
available December 2014,
only from Harlequin Intrigue.

HIEXP69800

HARLEQUIN®

INTRIGUE®

A DECADES-OLD COLD CASE IS TESTING EVERYTHING ONE TEXAS RANGER THOUGHT HE KNEW ABOUT OBTAINING JUSTICE...

A lot of men on death row profess their innocence. Those men are mostly just scared of dying. Jaxon Ward understands that, but as a Texas Ranger he needs to uphold the law. Yet the story Avery Tierney tells him...her story sounds true. Her brother is awaiting execution while the real killer remains at large. For twenty years the murderer has lived as a free man—and isn't eager to trade in his freedom.

Searching for the killer opens old wounds for Avery, and now she has to face a past so traumatic she blocked it out. A past not so disimilar to Jax's. Before long, the only comfort they find is in each other's arms. Avery knows it's dangerous to get too attached. After all, she's lost everything once before. And if she loses Jaxon, she fears she'll never recover.

COLD CASE IN CHEROKEE CROSSING

by RITA HERRON

Available December 2014,
wherever Harlequin® Intrigue® books and ebooks are sold.

www.Harlequin.com